In Praise of

BECOME THE ONLY CHOICE

A Customer-Focused Approach to Selling the Way People Buy

"Attitude, Personal Accountability, Perseverance and Habit. Mix in some strong process. It just doesn't get any better than that!"
- Aaron Grossman, Chief Executive Officer, TALENTLAUNCH

"This book is the foundation of our company's sales, client expansion and account retention approach and methodology. Read it and it will become the foundation of yours and you, too, will enjoy stellar results!"
- Frank J. Olivieri, President and COO, SupplyLogic

"I love the way Mike weaves in the lessons learned in athletics and ties them to sales. He makes it easy to learn sales process!"
- Terence Dixon, President, Konica Minolta

"Mike has a talent for taking complex concepts and presenting them in a way every sales person can understand and start implementing immediately. Read this book and become the only choice for your clients."
- John Falconetti, CEO, Drummond Press

MIKE JACOUTOT

Cover Design: Kate Jacoutot

Note for Librarians: a cataloguing record for this book that includes
Dewey Decimal Classification and US Library of Congress numbers is
available from the Library and Archives of Canada. The complete
cataloguing record can be obtained from their online database at:
www.collectionscanada.ca/amicus/index-e.html
ISBN 1-4120-4361-1

Acknowledgement

Writing a book may seem like a solitary effort, but it really is not. As I reflect on my life, I am reminded of the classic Christmas movie starring Jimmy Stewart — "It's a Wonderful Life." This movie is my all-time favorite and one that serves as a reminder to me of all the people who have touched my life.

I must start with my parents, Bill and Ellen Jacoutot, who taught me to stand on my own two feet and always encouraged me to be the best I could be. I grew up in a family as the middle child of seven. Each of my brothers and sisters helped to strengthen me as a person. Whether I admired their education, their dedication or had the opportunity to mentor them, my sincere thanks go to Ellie, Bill, Tom, Eileen, Kevin and Tim. Rest assured, your spirit is captured in this book.

From an athletic perspective, I have been blessed with two outstanding Hall of Fame coaches at the high school and collegiate level. Coach Greg DeMarco taught me about personal accountability. Coach Dave Icenhower gave me the opportunity to lead a national championship team and challenged me to get a little better every single day. I know they both thought they stopped coaching me the last day I wrestled for them, but nothing could be further from the truth. Their lessons are timeless, and I am truly thankful they were a part of my life.

My business life is one that has been touched by too many people to name. My thanks go to Al Batten, former Vice President Northeast Sales for Standard Register.

Al's stories are detailed throughout this book from "No one's shooting bullets at you" to "Thank God, I wasn't waiting for oxygen." Al was a great mentor to me in the early years, and his lessons have stayed with me.

As I moved from the sales field into the corporate office, I am very thankful to have had the opportunity to work under Joe Schwan, former Chief Operating Officer at Standard Register. Joe taught me many things; but most of all, he taught me that we are in the "customer business" first and foremost. At the end of the day, it's their belief in us that rewards us in the form of a paycheck.

As I moved up through the ranks, I could always count on two people to tell it like it is. First, my Butler Street partner and co-owner Mary Ann McLaughlin. Mary Ann has spent the last 20 years challenging me in a variety of ways and has established herself as my number one go-to person. While we have always debated issues enthusiastically, I honestly cannot think of another person I would choose to go to battle with. Mary Ann continually challenged me on strategy and sales process. Second, the late Frank Piperata, the very first person I ever hired, was always there with the people side, interjecting humor so that we never took ourselves too seriously.

Two other people who have played a critical part in shaping my sales approach are Neil Rackham and Jack Carew, both successful authors and leaders of sales effectiveness companies. Neil's knowledge of process and his diagnostically oriented approach influenced the basis for the SIGN effective questioning structure. Neil's breakthrough book "*SPIN Selling*" helped pave the way for the modern day consultative salesperson. Jack Carew is probably the best relationship-oriented salesperson I have ever met. Jack taught me to never underestimate the relationship side of the business. His relentless approach to finding an area of opportunity and working to continually solve customer problems had a tremendous impact on my professional career.

Jim Reese, former CEO of Randstad North America, gave me a wonderful opportunity to test my consultative selling approach by rolling the program out to a 1,300-person field sales and recruiting organization, and I think he would agree the results speak for themselves. I am deeply grateful for the opportunities he offered me.

To my wife, Kathy: your support means the world to me, and I couldn't have done it without you. It's not every day a husband quits a $300k+ a year job in 2004 and says he is going to write a book. You didn't bat an eye, saying, "if that is what you want to do." Thank you for believing in me.

To my kids, Michael, Bryan and Kaitlyn, having been raised on The Four Cornerstones of Success®, all three successful in their careers. I want to say that I am very proud of what you have already accomplished and the way each of you live your lives by those cornerstones.

Table of Contents

Introduction —
An Identification of Needs!

This book was written for you. Maybe you are in a bookstore seeking to improve your sales effectiveness, or perhaps you just heard me speak about how to sell effectively in today's increasingly competitive marketplace. Possibly, a friend or colleague suggested you read this book. Regardless of how you got to this page, you are at the "Identification of Needs" stage of the Buying/Decision Process. There is a GAP between what you believe is your desired state of performance — and your actual state of performance. In its simplest form, this "GAP" state is called an Identification of Needs. In other words, you — as a buyer — are at a "coachable moment," and I — as the seller — am in position to influence your buying behavior. There is an old saying, *"When the student is ready, the teacher appears."*

You may be new to sales and trying to understand how you can perform better, or you may be a seasoned veteran that has slipped into a selling rut. Perhaps, you are simply trying to take your craft to the next level and want to get a little bit better every day.

Whatever your aim, you have arrived at an "Identification of Needs." Whether buying a book, a car, or a new computer, all customer buying decisions start with an identification of needs. Customers have needs every single day. Customers have needs they may not even realize they have. Great salespeople find creative ways to meet those needs and effectively help customers understand their needs in new or different ways. Great salespeople meet this challenge every day through preparation, developing a thorough understanding of the Buying/Decision Process and understanding their customers' *operating reality*.

By reading this book, you will learn — and can put into practice — a set of strategies that will position you to hone your craft and become one of those great salespeople.

You will:

- Understand The Four Cornerstones of Success®

- Become more diagnostically oriented – seek to understand your customer before asking to be understood

- Focus on the accounts where you can create the highest value and truly understand that time is money — both for you and your customer

- Gain a greater understanding of the buying/ decision process and learn how to see problems and opportunities as they exist through your customers' eyes

- Use the SIGN questions — *Situation, Insight, GAP and Needs/Solution* — to create value for your customers

- Understand how to create an "Identification of

Needs" and how to move your customer through the buying/decision process

- Learn how to effectively handle customer objections

- How to plan and prepare to make an effective sales call

- Always know where you are in the Customer Relationship Pyramid

- Position yourself to become the ONLY Choice — the business will be yours to lose.

I hope you enjoy reading this book as much as I have enjoyed writing it. Now turn the page to go on this great sales journey with Frank and watch how his friend, Al, and a man known to many as simply "The Wizard," transform Frank into the salesperson he always knew he could be and help position him to *"Become the Only Choice"* with his customers.

Chapter 1:
O'Leary's Pub

There he sat on a bar stool in an old New York City landmark. O'Leary's Pub — which sat smack in the middle of New York's financial district. O'Leary's was a popular hangout for the under-thirty crowd and the place people came to unwind after work. It was Wednesday evening just past six o'clock on a cold February night. At the end of the bar, sitting apart from the other patrons, was a young man. One look at his face made clear that this was not a banner day for him.

Frank Kelly, a twenty-five-year-old salesman from the Standard Company, was alone, unhappy and patiently waiting for an old friend and former college teammate to meet him for a drink.

He had no way of knowing that this day — a day that did not appear to be going well at all — would have a profound effect on the rest of his career!

Frank started with Standard straight out of college. He chose Standard for two reasons: The company was in a growth industry and had a well-respected sales training program. Several other companies heavily recruited Frank during his senior year, two of them big name, Fortune 100 companies. Both made Frank offers, but he settled on Standard because he was convinced the culture and the training would offer an environment in which he could thrive.

Standard had just over $1 billion in annual revenues. In Frank's mind, Standard was big enough for him to benefit from its brand value and have significant resources at his disposal, yet small enough to afford him opportunities for personal growth faster than the two Fortune 100 companies.

Right out of college, Frank could pretty much write his own ticket. He was President of the university's Marketing Association, graduating with honors, and a 3.6 GPA.

In addition, Frank was quite an accomplished athlete and leader. He was a four-year varsity wrestler and captain of the wrestling team. He finished his senior year by winning the conference championship and went on to take second at the NCAA Championships. Frank was the successful student athlete that companies like Standard love to hire. You know the type — smart, competitive and with a hatred for failure. For most companies, these characteristics signify a strong sales profile.

Frank was coming off two relatively lackluster years in terms of sales performance as he was closing in on wrapping up his third full-year with the company. All through college his friends repeatedly assured him he would be a great salesperson. He was smart, funny, friendly and seemed to genuinely care about people. "A perfect combination to be a great salesperson," they told him again and again.

Yet on this night, Frank was sitting alone on a bar stool

in New York City's financial district in a very unfamiliar position. He was feeling like a failure, "crying in his beer". It seemed like a lifetime away from the position of pride he felt when standing on the podium earning All-American honors only three short years earlier.

"How could this happen again?" he asked himself. *"How could I lose another deal? I was certain this one was going to go my way! This makes three in a row... a three-time loser this year already."*

At that exact moment, Frank's good friend and mentor Al Marion walked through the door. Frank didn't see Al come in, but Al noticed Frank right away – looking melancholy, sitting alone and all the way at the other end of the bar.

"How's it going Frank?" Al asked as he greeted his former teammate and good friend. "Hey Al, I'm *doin'* all right. How you *doin'*?" Frank asked with his deep New York accent. "Can I get you a beer?"

"I'm *doin'* good," said Al, his New York accent still intact as well. "Yeah, I'll have a beer."

Frank signaled to the bartender for two beers as Al sat on the stool next to him.

Frank had been looking forward to seeing Al this cold February evening. You see, they went back a long way. Al had been Frank's good friend and mentor for the past seven years. Al was a senior in college when they first met, and Frank remembered it like it was yesterday.

It was the first day of wrestling practice in Frank's freshman year. Al was captain of the team and was a three-time All-American — finishing second in the nationals three years in a row and triply determined to not let the elusive national title escape him in his senior year.

Frank had heard all about Al — his reputation for being a good natured but no-nonsense type of guy and the scuttlebutt that he might end up being the first four-time national runner-up in NCAA history. A title by most people's standards would be awesome, but anyone who knew Al knew that it would not sit well with him. Al would have considered himself a four-time loser. Those close to Al would have none of that four-time runner-up talk during his senior year and rightfully so.

Ultimately, his focus, determination, and discipline enabled Al to breeze through the national tournament, pinning all five wrestlers he faced and winning his first national title on his way to becoming the university's first four-time All-American. In the spring of his senior year, Al gained tremendous notoriety, becoming what his friends called the BMOC — big man on campus! Frank always looked up to Al not only as an athlete and a leader, but he also had tremendous respect for Al's ability as a salesperson. In fact, one of the primary reasons Frank decided to join Standard was to be on the same team as his mentor, once again.

Although Al had transferred to Philadelphia nearly three and a half years before, he and Frank made it a practice to speak to each other at least once a week. Al had been one of the top salespeople at Standard for the prior two years after a relatively slow start himself.

Being a good mentor, Al sensed that his friend was struggling the last time they had spoken, so he decided to pay him a visit when he was in New York to meet with a couple of the demanding committee members from his hottest prospect, The Reliant Company.

Al turned to Frank and looked straight into his eyes as though he were searching for something. "So...how's it really going, Frank?" he asked, sensing that Frank wanted to share something with him. "You don't look like you have your usual cherub-like demeanor going for you today. What's the matter?"

 Frank hesitated for a moment. He seriously considered not sharing yet another disappointing outcome with his friend Al as he looked in his eyes — but only for a few seconds. Frank knew he couldn't hide this disappointment from his friend and mentor, and after careful consideration decided to give it to him straight.

"Honestly, I am not doing so well. I lost another deal," Frank confessed — his voice trailing off just as he uttered the bitter words.

"You what?" Al inquired, unable to make out all of Frank's words.

"I lost the Lassiter deal," Frank said. "You remember me telling you about the Lassiter deal, don't you? It was the

$1.5 million deal I have been working on for the past six months. "I thought for sure that deal was mine...all the signs were there."

Al could see the pain on Frank's face. "What do you mean 'all the signs were there'?" asked Al. "What signs, Frank? That is if you don't mind me asking."

"No, of course, I don't mind you asking. We had a great initial meeting with terrific rapport. I thought they really liked me. They said they knew Standard had the capability to handle the program and they believed I did a good job with the presentation," offered Frank. "I have no idea what went wrong." Frank's confusion and state of shock were evident from his woeful expression.

"Did they give you a reason why they didn't choose Standard?" asked a genuinely concerned, Al.

"They sure did," Frank responded. "They said that with all things considered, our price was too high and they could not justify the difference." Frank turned away long enough to take a sip of his beer and then turned back toward Al. "I've got to tell you, Al; our prices really are a problem. I am always losing deals because of price. This company needs to work harder to get its overall costs in line or I am telling you, they are going to start losing some talented salespeople."

Al took a slow sip of his beer while he thought about what Frank had just said.

Before Al could respond to his tirade about the

company's pricing practices, Frank continued, "I was talking to Steve Adams and Bonnie Wright earlier in the week, and they were complaining that our costs have gotten totally out of line. The two of them are seriously considering looking elsewhere."

"So… Steve and Bonnie are considering leaving the company because our prices are too high. Is that what I heard you say?" asked Al in disbelief.

"Yes, that is **absolutely right**!" snapped Frank in a tone out of character for him. "And the two of them are pretty talented salespeople in my book."

"First of all, Frank, if we are truly honest here, Steve and Bonnie are average salespeople at best. But going back to your statement, do you honestly believe that you are losing all these deals because our prices are too high?" The tone of Al's voice clearly showed he was beginning to move into mentor mode.

 "You do the math, Al. If everybody is losing deals and the customers are all telling us it is because our prices are too high, then maybe — just maybe — we should listen to them and make some adjustments!" By this time, Frank had convinced himself that the company's prices were the reason for his lack of success.

Time for Tough Love

Al listened intently, sensing the frustration in Frank's voice. He understood that Frank was having a tough time and knew his long-time friend needed his help.

But could Al give him all the help he needed? It was nearly 6:30 PM and he only had about another hour and a half before he had to leave to catch the 8:40 train back to Philadelphia.

Al had an important meeting with the Reliant Company in the morning. He had spent the day in Reliant's New York office gaining a better understanding of the needs and wants of two of their most demanding users. Starting the all-important relationship building process with them, Al was investing the time to make sure he understood the needs and wants of these two committee members who happened to be located in New York. The Reliant deal was worth nearly $4 million annually, and he felt confident after today's meeting that he had positioned himself and Standard as the only choice in the customer's eyes.

Al was already a three-time member of the President's Roundtable — an award reserved for the top ten salespeople in the company. He also knew the Reliant deal would easily push him to #1 nationally. While this was a familiar place for Al in sports, it was a position he hadn't been in since he stepped off the podium nearly seven years ago. While he recognized he didn't have time to give Frank all the help he needed tonight, he knew he could certainly get him started by helping Frank understand The Four Cornerstones of Success®: *Attitude, Personal Accountability, Perseverance and Habit.*

Al flashed back to years ago when he, too, was struggling in his sales career, questioning if he could make it as a sales professional. Fortunately, he blossomed, thanks to the help he received from his mentor — a man the people at Standard simply referred to as "The Wizard." Given the time he had left with Frank was short, he decided he would make arrangements for Frank to spend some time with The Wizard as soon as possible. Al determined that in the brief time he had with Frank, the most important thing he could do was to bring Frank to a coachable moment so that The Wizard could take it from there. Al knew Frank had the potential to join him at the President's Roundtable. He also knew The Wizard was an expert in assisting people to reach their potential as top-notch sales professionals.

After Frank's little temper tantrum, Al decided it might be better for the two to order dinner at the bar and indulge in a little bit of a "coachable moment," just like they did back in the good old days. You see, coming out of high school Frank was an accomplished athlete himself. He was a two-time state champion and was unaccustomed to losing. So, when he stepped into the university's wrestling room his freshman year and realized he would be starting, Frank thought things would be just like high school — where he won nearly 98% of the time.

Unfortunately, things did not turn out that way. While he did start varsity as a freshman, he was just another high school state champion trying to make it at a collegiate level. Former high school state champions are a dime a dozen at the collegiate level in many sports. Wrestling was no exception.

Frank had a tough time making the transition to collegiate wrestling. While he experienced no losses during his high school junior and senior years and won state titles both years, he started his collegiate campaign with no wins for the first five matches and was pinned for the first time in his life! He became very frustrated and lost his confidence. After his fifth straight loss, Al, being the team captain and seeing Frank's inherent potential, took it upon himself to offer Frank a pep talk. Al told Frank he shouldn't worry and reassured him that it was not unusual for any freshman to have a tough time making the transition to collegiate wrestling. Al vividly remembered Frank's response to that pep talk.

Because losing was a relatively new experience for him, Frank failed to take responsibility for his performance and blamed everything and anyone he could for his personal losing streak. His immaturity was clearly evident that day, and Frank's response didn't sit well with the team captain. Al decided to give his wet-behind-the-ears teammate his first lesson on personal accountability — a lesson that went a long way toward helping Frank make the adjustments necessary to enable him to regain his confidence and put his athletic career back on track.

As he remembered Frank's reaction back then, he realized he heard the same reaction just a few minutes ago, when Frank was complaining about the company's pricing practices. Was Frank again losing confidence in himself? Was his attitude starting to go bad? As a former athlete and a top salesperson, Al could relate to the frustration Frank was feeling. He knew his friend needed help — and knew he needed it now.

Chapter 2: The Four Cornerstones of Success

Cornerstone #1: Attitude

As Frank was taking a long sip of his beer, Al started with his version of Mentoring 101.

"Frank," Al began, "I haven't seen you with an attitude this bad since you started your freshman year 0-5. What's with all the negativity?" Al was trying to understand whether Frank knew that his attitude was his biggest problem.

"My attitude is bad?" Frank snapped. "Oh, I am sorry — I am not Al Marion! I am not a four-time All-American and three-time President's Roundtable member! I am not Mr. Perfect! I am just a has-been athlete that can't seem to sell my way out of a paper bag!" Even Frank was shocked at how easily the sarcasm rolled off his tongue. Judging by the look on Al's face, Frank realized he needed to tone things down a bit. And he did.

"Al," Frank continued in a milder tone. "I appreciate you taking the time to meet with me and I am sorry I am not the salesperson you expected me to be. But I am not the wet-behind-the-ears' kid you saved years ago. I am a grown man who has been out in the business world for nearly three years, and the fact is... I am just not making it!"

Al took a long look at his friend, seeing the pain and frustration on his face gave him pause to go slowly. But then again, that wasn't Al's style.

"Frank, I can appreciate the fact that you are struggling. I can also appreciate the fact that it is causing you a great deal of pain. But you need to take a mental dump and let the negative attitude go."

"WHAT?" asked Frank. "WHAT DID YOU SAY?"

"I said, you need to take a mental dump and let the negative attitude go," replied Al, with a slight grin.

"MENTAL DUMP?" said Frank in disbelief, as he let out a half-hearted chuckle. "Where on earth did you come up with that term? You think that's what is causing me to lose deals? Because if that's the case, there must be some sort of 'mental laxative' I can take to make things all better!" Frank was now bringing his negativity to a fevered pitch as he reached for another handful of pretzels.

"You know what I mean," said Al in a calm, reassuring tone. "It's a sort of constipation of the mind. It blocks you from allowing yourself to see the positive side of things."

Frank just stared at Al, still trying to understand the term "mental dump" and where he was going with it…

"In a lot of ways, Frank, sales *is* like wrestling," Al continued, "Selling requires a tremendous amount of psychological endurance; you have to persist until the deal is done. You must conquer your fears and, like wrestling, there are starts and stops —wins and losses. New decision-makers can come in the middle of the process and change the rules of the game. Salespeople are highly visible within the company. You are constantly exposed to the possibility of rejection. All your successes and failures can be easily viewed on the monthly quota board. And guess what? It can get darn lonely when you are not achieving your goals! Yes, that's right...pats on the back are few and far between when you're not making your numbers. You must think of yourself as an integral part of the revenue-generating engine that keeps this company running. That's a massive load for people like us to carry and that is why attitude is so important."

"I am a big believer in the effects of attitude," Al continued. "Everything you've accomplished or failed to accomplish in life started with your attitude. I know some people say attitude is everything. And while I'm not certain that's an absolute, I do believe that attitude is the gate to the mind and the start of everything that comes after. Attitude sets the tone for everything else you do."

Al took a deep breath before continuing. "A simple way of thinking about it is this: Some people see thunderstorms...other people look for rainbows. Some people see the glass as half empty...others see the opportunities associated with the glass as half full. Some people see icy streets...other people see the opportunity and put on ice skates. It all depends on how you look at things. Just like you did when you picked yourself up and dusted yourself off seven years ago, you need to find it within yourself to look for the positives and the opportunities in every situation. They are there if only you will allow yourself to see them."

Now Frank was confused. He thought for a minute about what Al was saying. *"Thunderstorms? Rainbows? Icy streets?*

"So, what you are saying, Al, is that I have to figure out a way to put on ice skates, right? Not a bad analogy, since I will more than likely miss quota AGAIN this month and I will really be on 'thin ice' with my boss!" His sarcasm was moving back into high gear again as the bartender approached to ask if they would be eating dinner at the bar.

"Yes," said Frank, realizing he had spoken for Al. Ironically, he was also beginning to realize that he enjoyed having Al mentor him again, helping him to work through a difficult patch.

He looked at Al and asked, "Is it ok? Do you have the time to have a quick bite? I would appreciate you staying; since I rarely have the opportunity to spend quality time with you."

While Al had had every intention of having dinner with his good friend, he was nonetheless flattered by Frank's need to talk things through with him and felt good about the way Frank had posed the question. Even though Frank was still showing signs of frustration, Al felt that he was beginning to come around and move toward that "coachable moment" he was trying so hard to establish.

Al looked at the bartender and simply said, "Two menus please."

He glanced at his watch and realized he only had an hour and fifteen minutes to create that coachable moment for his friend and to turn him over to The Wizard for the next stage of his journey.

"What time is your train?" asked Frank.

"8:40."

"You will need to be out of here by eight o'clock to be safe," said Frank.

"Yeah, I know," Al said. "We've got plenty of time." Even though Al was pleased that Frank wanted to spend more quality time with him, he still wasn't sure he was on the right track in getting Frank to understand that he needed to come to grips with his negative attitude, first and foremost. As the bartender came to take their order, Al knew they would have to make some significant headway between the salad and the main course. Frank ordered first.

"I'll have the chicken sandwich with fries."

"Would you like a salad with that?" asked the bartender.

"Yes," said Frank, "with Thousand Island on the side."

"How about you?" said the bartender, looking at Al.

"I'll have the same," Al said. "I could probably do without the fries, but I am sure it will motivate me to run in the morning."

"What are you worried about?" kidded Frank. "You're in phenomenal shape!"

"Yeah, maybe, but I have to run six days a week to keep it that way. Fries and beers tend to work against me staying that way," offered Al, as Frank nodded and smiled in agreement.

After a moment of awkward silence, "So, you think I need an attitude adjustment?" Frank asked. His comment came across as sort of a peace offering, since he had obviously given his mentor a little attitude a couple of minutes before.

Al decided to take the "memory lane" approach, walking Frank back to his freshman year in college rather than focusing on the string of recent deals that had gone south.

"Okay, so take a walk down memory lane with me," said Al. "You started your collegiate career 0-5, losing more matches in your first month of the season than you did your last three years in high school. I come over to give you a little pep talk and you lashed out at me by blaming everything and everyone around you for your shortcomings. Do you remember the one question I asked you then?"

"Yes. You asked me to share the positives about the situation you were in."

"And do you remember your response?" asked Al.

"Yes. I said I guess I know now what doesn't work," replied Frank.

"Exactly. And do you remember what I told you then?"

"Yes. You said the only thing good about losing is that

you learn where you are weak. And the good thing about that is that you learn where you need to improve," recalled Frank. "And then you turned and walked away."

"Right," confirmed Al. "Think about that experience and apply the same principles to sales and losing those deals.

The positive side of where you are today is that you have a tremendous opportunity to learn the areas where you need improvement. So, lesson number one is..." Al paused, "At the risk of history repeating itself, I am going to have to turn and walk away. I need to go to the men's room."

Before he left, he handed Frank a card, saying. "This is something a friend of mine gave me a little over three years ago, and it has helped me tremendously." The card said simply:

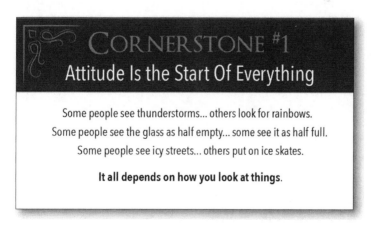

CORNERSTONE #1
Attitude Is the Start Of Everything

Some people see thunderstorms... others look for rainbows.
Some people see the glass as half empty... some see it as half full.
Some people see icy streets... others put on ice skates.

It all depends on how you look at things.

Frank stared at the card. He must have read it ten times, and thought to himself, *"This is so simple and so obvious. How could I possibly have missed this? My attitude is blurring my thinking. I am much better than this!"* As he started to put the card in his wallet, he noticed there was writing on the back of the card as well.

"Wow!" Frank thought to himself. *"Al has this card memorized! I'll give him credit: he really does believe attitude is the start of everything!"*

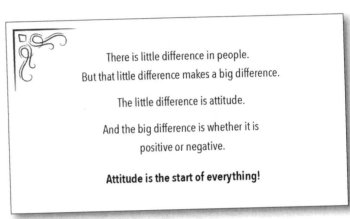

There is little difference in people.
But that little difference makes a big difference.

The little difference is attitude.

And the big difference is whether it is positive or negative.

Attitude is the start of everything!

Frank could feel his own attitude starting to change. He felt good about having his friend and mentor taking the time to help him tackle his current challenges. It hardly seemed possible that less than an hour ago, Frank was wallowing in self-pity. Suffering from the old *ain't it awfuls*. Now he was starting to feel better and was looking forward to Al's return. When Al did return a few moments later, Frank asked him where he had gotten the card.

"From MY mentor."

Al's reply generated a surprised look.

"You have a mentor? Why would *you* need a mentor? You're Al Marion. You're great at everything! You don't need a mentor! What's his name? Do I know him?"

"No," said Al. "You don't know him. And by the way, *everyone* needs a mentor, someone they can look to for advice and development. My mentor is a stand-out person. He is a tremendous sales guy, and an even better leader! He retired last month at 55 after 30 years in sales and sales management. People who have worked with him and know him well call him 'The Wizard' because he can make the most complex things seem simple, easy to learn and understand. I want you to meet with him next week. I think it would be good for you."

"That would be AWESOME!" exclaimed Frank. "Thanks a lot. Al." The sincerity in his face clearly reflected his excitement and genuine appreciation.

"If you don't mind me asking, how did you happen to meet him?"

"I met him just over three years ago, when I moved to Philadelphia. He had moved there just three months earlier to rebuild the district. He was my district manager. Standard used to move him around every two to three years, assigning him the underperforming Districts. Philadelphia happened to be the worst in the company at the time. One Friday afternoon, I came back to the office from another brutal day in the field after having one of the worst weeks in my professional career. It seemed that every order either shipped late or had a quality problem. I had a voice mailbox full of irate and disappointed customers. I had gotten through about half of the voice mails when I hung up the phone and just sat there with my head in my hands.

The Wizard sees me that way and asks, 'What's the problem?'.

"I immediately recited a laundry list of issues, ranging from late deliveries to quality problems. I can remember distinctly that he had an unlit, partially chewed cigar in his right hand, and he looked at me as though he could feel my pain. After about five minutes of listening to me whine, I stopped speaking and just looked at the man everyone called The Wizard, waiting for him to say something..."

"How old are you?" he asked in a very stern, staff-sergeant like voice.

"I am twenty-five, sir," I replied.

"Do you know where I was when I was twenty-five, son?" he asked.

I awkwardly replied "No, sir." Somehow, I felt like my world was going to begin to get rocked shortly.

"I was in a foxhole in Vietnam, with the North Vietnamese shooting bullets at me. Is anyone shooting bullets at you, son?" he asked, rhetorically.

"No sir."

"Then I suggest you put these problems into perspective," he said, as he put that slightly chewed cigar back in his mouth.

"Yes sir," I sheepishly replied, feeling like he must have

thought I was the most whiney, negative, self-centered idiot in the world!

"Follow me to my office," demanded The Wizard.

"As I reached his office, he took a card out of a cardholder on his desk. It was the attitude card I just gave you. As he gave it to me, he pointed to a saying posted on his wall.

Tough times never last. Tough people do.

And he said to me that day, "Everything you will ever succeed or fail at will begin with your attitude. Attitude is the start of everything. Now go take care of your customers."

"Wow!" said Frank. "After hearing that story, I am mortified I took the string of lost deals so badly. I can't believe I was so bummed out about things. I guess I was whining, too, huh?" When do you think I can meet The Wizard?"

"Let's take it a step at a time," cautioned Al.

Just then, the bartender brought the salads and Al and Frank began to eat. There was silence for about forty-five seconds, which seemed like an eternity to Frank. Not knowing where Al was taking the discussion, Frank decided (wisely) that he would wait for Al to start the conversation back up.

"So… you are losing deals on price, are you?" asked Al, seemingly sympathetic and genuinely interested in helping Frank get the pricing problem fixed.

"That's what the customers are telling me," Frank replied quickly, after taking another bite of salad.

"First it was the Sprayberry Industries deal, then the Walton deal, and now the Lassiter deal. In each one of these cases, the customer said they could not justify our pricing, and they went with a lower cost alternative."

"Was that exactly what the customers said?" asked Al, apparently unconvinced. "They said they went with a lower cost alternative?" It was clear he was taking the discussion somewhere.

"Yes," said Frank, "more or less."

"Those are mystery words to me, Frank. What do you mean, 'more or less'? What pricing level did you quote?" asked Al.

"Standard volume discounts with incentives for early pay," answered Frank.

"That's what I typically quote," offered Al. "Less the incentives for early pay."

"What's your point, Al?" asked an increasingly defensive Frank. He wasn't sure he liked where the discussion was headed.

"The point is, I sell with the same prices as you and I am winning deals," answered Al. "Our pricing is virtually the same across the entire company. Seven hundred reps are selling with the same cost base and the same mark-ups."

"Well, that pricing may work in Philadelphia. But

New York City is a different and more competitive market." Frank contended as his justification skills were kicking in.

"I am quite familiar with the New York market, Frank. Remember, I sold in New York up until three short years ago."

"And as I recall, you did not make the President's Roundtable while you were selling in New York, did you?" countered Frank. This was a question to which Frank clearly knew the answer.

"That is correct, Frank. I did not make the President's Roundtable while I was selling in New York. However, I did make 100 Plus Club."

100 Plus Club was an annual recognition conference for salespeople and managers who had achieved a minimum of 100% of their targets. Al was willing to concede the fact he did not make the President's Roundtable, but not the point of the discussion. If he let Frank off the hook by allowing him to rationalize that his market was tougher, then his time with The Wizard would surely be wasted.

"Frank," Al began, "I may not have made the President's Roundtable while selling in New York, but Mary Ann McManus and Mike Chicetti make the Roundtable every year, and both work in New York City. And, guess what? They are selling with the same prices you are selling with every single day."

Al's response was 100% fact-based and Frank knew it.

Mary Ann and Mike were selling with the same prices and were making it big in New York City. Mike and Mary Ann worked in different offices than Frank. Mary Ann worked for a manager named Morgan Chalk, and Mike worked for a manager named Janet Dorring. Both managers were seasoned veterans and frequent members of Standard's 100 Plus Club.

Frank had spent time with both Mary Ann and Mike at one of Standard's northeast sales meetings and remembered coming away not overly impressed with either one of them.

"They weren't silver-tongued or dynamic or anything like that," Frank thought to himself. "How can they be winning in the New York marketplace while I am not? It has to be their management." Frank was an expert at finding external reasons for his lack of success, and this situation was no different.

"True," said Frank, as he collected his thoughts. "But I don't have the benefit of working for top managers like Morgan Chalk or Janet Dorring. I mean, Fred is a good guy," Frank said, referring to his manager Fred Wilson. "But he's no Morgan Chalk."

Al thought to himself, "This is really irritating. What has happened to my friend? He doesn't seem willing to take responsibility for anything. The prices are too high! The market is different! He doesn't have the best manager! Next thing you know, he will be telling me the economy is bad!"

As the bartender came to take away the salad plates, Al was thinking back to their teammate days to find a situation in Frank's past wrestling career where he was able to turn himself around and be the All-American wrestler he knew he could be. It didn't take long for Al to find that familiar spot.

"Frank, remember when you started the year 0-5,..."

Frank quickly interrupted. "Oh, no, here we go again. You're not going to beat that tired old dog again, are you?" questioned Frank, in disbelief.

"I believe I am," confessed Al. "That period was a defining moment where you lost your confidence and you were seriously considering quitting the team.

I can see that happening all over again. This situation is really no different."

"So, you're afraid I am going to quit Standard?" asked Frank.

"No. I am afraid you are going to quit on Frank," Al said sharply. Just then, the bartender brought their dinner and asked if they wanted another round, giving Frank a moment to get his thoughts around what his friend had just said to him.

"No thanks," said Frank. "Um, but I will have a glass of ice water."

"Make it two," said Al. "And can we have some ketchup?" The bartender walked away and returned with two glasses of ice water, forgetting the ketchup.

Cornerstone #2: Personal Accountability

As Al stood up to retrieve a bottle of ketchup from one of the tables behind him, he reached in his pocket and handed Frank his second card. The card simply read:

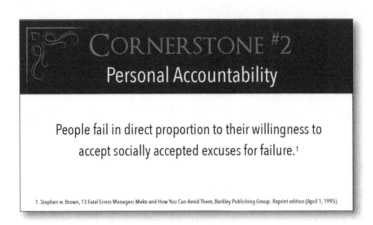

CORNERSTONE #2
Personal Accountability

People fail in direct proportion to their willingness to accept socially accepted excuses for failure.[1]

1. Stephen w. Brown, 13 Fatal Errors Managers Make and How You Can Avoid Them, Berkley Publishing Group, Reprint edition (April 1, 1995).

Frank read the card but did not understand what Al was driving at.

"What does he mean by 'socially accepted excuses'?" he thought to himself. "Does he think I am a failure?"

Al returned to the bar, but, before he could sit down, Frank was on the attack.

"What does this card mean, Al? Are you saying I am a failure? Are you saying I am making excuses?" Frank asked aggressively.

"Frank," Al replied in a relaxed and reassuring tone, "I don't think you're a failure. I do think, however, that you are becoming comfortable with some of the more socially accepted excuses for failure."

"What the hell does that mean?" asked Frank. His concerned tone of voice reflected a trace of self-doubt. "I don't think I make excuses. I am stating facts. Do you really think I make excuses, Al?"

Frank was starting to get a very uneasy feeling in his stomach. He knew he was about to cross a line with his friend. And he knew there was no turning back from this conversation. Nevertheless, he was not anxious to hear Al's response.

The thought of letting Frank off easily had crossed Al's mind, if only for a moment. He knew now was the time to be the true mentor Frank needed. The fact was, Frank was failing and it was no accident. He was struggling with his attitude and he was not accepting personal accountability for his poor performance. If Al was going to make an impact on his friend, it was now or never.

Al began, choosing his words carefully.

"Let me share something with you, Frank. Spending the past three years under The Wizard and most of my life around athletics, I have learned that there is a direct relationship between failure and excuses, just like I have learned there is a direct relationship between personal accountability and success. Essentially, there are two actions in life — performance or excuses. You need to decide right now which one you are going to demand of yourself and from those with whom you work."

As Al stopped speaking, he could see anger and defensiveness in Frank's expression.

"But Al, it's not like I am not trying!" Frank countered in frustration.

Al was not going to let his friend off the hook, even though he was concerned there could be lasting damage to their relationship. This was a critical stage in the conversation — and the mentoring that Al had set out to provide.

"Trying is just a noisy way of not doing something!" Al spoke sharply and to the point, not giving Frank an out.

"Either you do it or you don't. Either you win the deal, or you don't. There is no medal for trying. If you are going to get the most out of your visit with The Wizard, you need to start with the right attitude, and you need to start being accountable for your actions, your inaction, and your failures."

"Read that card again, Frank." Al spoke in a strong, commanding tone that left Frank no option but to obey.

He began to read the card again, this time out loud. "People fail in direct proportion to their willingness to accept socially accepted excuses for failure."

While Frank was reading, he was also thinking how his good friend, Al, was being awfully tough on him. After all, this was supposed to be a friendly, casual get-together between two old friends. Frank was becoming more and more irritated with Al's position on this whole "socially accepted excuses" thing.

"Do you know what is meant by the term 'socially accepted excuse'?" Al asked.

"No," responded Frank in an almost insubordinate tone, "But, I have a strong feeling you are going to educate me."

"You can start by turning the card over," Al said. "Start reading the excuses listed on the card, from top to bottom. Frank read the back of the card as instructed and was starting to understand this concept of "socially accepted excuses." It gave him a sick feeling in his stomach. He knew the answer to the question he was about to ask, but he felt the need to ask it, anyway.

SOCIALLY ACCEPTABLE EXCUSES
1. I would get the order, but our prices are too high.
2. I would be on quota if it weren't for the economy.
3. I would be successful it there was more time in a day.
4. I would be good if I had a better territory.
5. I would be successful if I had more education.
6. I would really be making it if I had a product to sell.
7. I would be achieving my quota if the competition would stop undercutting me!
8. I would be successful if my boss would support me.
9. I would be happier if my family would support me.
10. I would be making it if I worked for a different company.

"Do I say these things, Al?" asked Frank. His voice trailed off, showing the beginnings of disappointment in himself.

"As much as it pains me to say, Frank: yes, you do. I believe I heard #1, #4, #7 and #8 in the last hour alone. And at your current pace, it probably won't be too long before #10 hits your radar screen," responded Al, uncompromisingly.

"I see," replied a suddenly crestfallen, Frank. He was facing for the first time, the realization that the excuses flowed easily from his own mouth.

"I have adopted these socially accepted excuses, haven't I, Al?"

The conversation was not an easy one for Al.

"Frank, not totally, but you are beginning to adopt some very bad habits, like being comfortable with socially accepted excuses. Everyone has moments when they wallow in self-pity, but you must not let these bad habits become the norm. Bad habits are like comfortable beds. They are easy to get into and difficult to get out of. People who use statements like these are taking the position that they are not in control of their lives. I call them victims. Everything happens to them — they have convinced themselves that they have no control over anything! The prices are bad, the economy is bad, the training is bad, and their family is bad. These people accept no personal accountability for their actions, inaction — or for their failures. What they want you to believe is that the prices are too high and it's the prices that are failing, not them."

 "And all this is in spite of the fact that there are a hundred-other people in the company that are extremely successful selling with the same prices. If everyone truly held themselves accountable, they would say something like: 'Until I can create enough value for the customer to justify my price, I will not be successful.' This would cause them to think long and hard about what they are doing — to truly understand what is working and what's not working; What mistakes they have made; what adjustments they need to make. A good investment for these 'victims' would be to buy a mirror and take a real hard look at the person who is handicapping their success."

"So, I should take a long, hard look in the mirror?" asked Frank. "Is that what you are saying?"

"Yes. It should be the first place you look every time you fail," Al replied emphatically. "Hey, it happens to all of us from time to time."

"Yeah, it happens to all of us regular guys," said Frank, clearly sulking. "It just doesn't happen to people like you."

"That's just not true, Frank. It happens to everyone. Let me tell you a story. Several years ago, I had the pleasure of working with The Wizard on a big opportunity. He had just come to Philadelphia but was still living in Chicago, going home every weekend. It was Friday afternoon, and I had a big presentation with Kell Semiconductor. In my mind, this account had a tremendous amount of potential."

"One of the things The Wizard always preached about customer presentations was not leaving anything to chance. 'Get in the room where you will be presenting the night before,' he would say. Test your technology. Make sure the Internet connection works for your demo. Bring a set of screen prints of the demo in case the server goes down. Bring a back-up printed set of slides for everyone. Bring an extra bulb for your projector. Control what you can control. Plan for the worst and even if there is a problem, the customer will know you anticipated it and were prepared to make the adjustments."

"Well, to make a long story short, we didn't get in the room the night before, the Internet connection didn't work, we didn't have screen shots of the demo and we fell flat on our face. The saddest part of this story is that that wasn't the worst part. The drive with The Wizard to the airport was even worse. I had to spend that 45 minutes answering one question after another from him about preparation and execution. At first, I — like most people — tried to rationalize that it was the customer's fault for not allowing us in the room the night before. When I saw he wasn't buying it and that he was holding me accountable — that's when the coachable moment began. Today I am one of the most successful salespeople in the company, and you can bet I hold everyone who works with me accountable for their actions and inactions. It was a great lesson The Wizard taught me that day:

Good judgment comes from experience, and experience comes from bad judgment.

"It makes perfect sense, Al," confessed Frank. "But what can I do to change? This is a bit frightening. Clearly, you were able to change. I'm not sure where to start."

"Yes, I was able to change. The Wizard taught me that I needed to start by trying to find the positive in every situation. Once I did that, the next thing I had to come to grips with was being able to hold myself accountable for my results. Any time I lost a deal going forward, I would say to myself, 'I was OUTSOLD...and these are the necessary adjustments I need to make so that it won't happen again.' The first time I was able to actually take that position was clearly a defining moment in my sales career."

"Frank, you lost the Lassiter deal. What happened?"

"I thought we discussed this," replied a confused Frank.

"Why did you lose?" Al asked in a commanding tone. "And don't say your prices were too high!"

Frank was a little taken aback by Al's strong tone, but understood what Al was trying to accomplish.

"I got outsold," said a reflective Frank.

"Good. And what adjustments will you make going forward?"

"I will do a better job understanding who the key decision makers and key decision influencers are and gain a clear line of sight into critical concerns and objectives."

"Excellent answer, Frank. I hope this will be your defining moment."

"My defining moment?" asked Frank.

"Yes," replied Al, thinking back. "That is a point in time where you reach a crossroad from where you can look back and see that the decision or decisions you made that day had a significant impact on your life."

"Do you think this is my defining moment?" asked Frank, quietly.

"If not a defining moment, certainly a coachable moment," chuckled Al.

"Let's just say a coachable moment is a given," Frank conceded. "So, let me make sure that I can summarize your thoughts on personal accountability:

1. Understand need for personal accountability and refrain from using socially accepted excuses

2. Get a grip on the fact that essentially in life there are two actions: performance and excuses

3. And anytime I lose a deal, I need to admit that I was outsold and define what adjustments I need to make going forward."

"You've got it!" beamed Al, as a big smile came over his face.

Al felt great seeing that his friend was really beginning to come around, and he was quite proud of himself for being able to get through to him.

"Let me ask you a question, Al." said Frank. "Would you say that a positive attitude and personal accountability are the keys to *your* success?"

"It is not just limited to those two," replied Al, giving the matter some thought. "But they are two of *The Four Cornerstones of Success*® necessary to take you to the next level."

"Two of four cornerstones?" asked Frank. "What are the other two?"

Just then, the bartender appeared to ask if the two of them wanted coffee, as he took their dinner plates away.

"How are you doing on time?" Frank asked.

"It's 7:30 now, so I have a half hour," replied Al, checking his watch. "I have time for coffee. How about you?"

"I'm all ears, Al! Bring on the coffee! And bring on Cornerstones 3 & 4!" exclaimed Frank.

Al was pleased that Frank was finally coming around. It was tough having this type of conversation with his good friend. Frank had a lot of talent — just as he did in his freshman year of college. He just needed a little coaching and mentoring to show him the way. Al also knew he had only 30 minutes left to get Frank ready for his meeting with The Wizard.

The Wizard did not have the time nor the patience to teach Frank *The Four Cornerstones of Success*®. The Wizard expected that people would come to him with those basics in place. With the progress they were already making, Al was certain he could help Frank get to the next level. He needed to help him get his head on straight so that he would get the most out of his time with The Wizard.

"So, you want Cornerstone Number Three?" Al asked, in a mentoring sort of way.

"Bring it on, Al! I am ready for Cornerstone Number Three!" said Frank, enthusiastically pounding his fists on the bar like a little kid waiting for a piece of candy.

Cornerstone #3: Perseverance

So, Al pressed on. "The third cornerstone is perseverance..."

"Perseverance?" asked a perplexed Frank.

"You mean like: If at first you don't succeed...try, try again? Because if it is, I've heard that before. That's certainly not rocket science."

"In a way, yes...in a way, no," Al countered.

Sensing that his friend was disappointed with the third cornerstone, Al's voice took on a more reassuring tone. He knew that this was a delicate moment and that he could lose Frank and all that he had accomplished with the first two cornerstones. He knew he only had a short window of opportunity to communicate his point and have Frank walk away prepared and mentally ready to have his own "defining moment" with The Wizard. Al reached in his pocket and handed Frank a third card, and printed on it was the following:

> *"Progressive Improvement...is better than Postponed Perfection."*

Frank first read the card to himself, and then quietly read the card aloud: "Progressive improvement is better than postponed perfection."

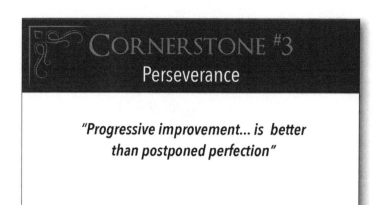

"Do you understand what that means, Frank?"

"I think so...uh, maybe," replied Frank with uncertainty.

"Think back to your wrestling days again, Frank. Remember what Coach Ice used to tell us?" Al thought back fondly to their college wrestling coach.

"Uh, no. Not really." Frank was still staring at the card, trying to grasp its meaning.

"Come on, Frank!" Al said more forcefully. "What did Coach say at the beginning of every practice?"

This time Frank listened, understanding Al's question for the first time. He flashed back to his college days and pictured himself sitting cross-legged on the cold, somewhat hard wrestling mat. As he continued the flashback, the words Coach Ice said at the start of practice every day clearly came back to him:

Good afternoon, gentlemen — and I do use the term

loosely! Welcome to my world. For the next two hours, my goal is a simple one and my goal has not changed for twenty years! My goal is to make each and every one of you at least a little better than you were yesterday, but not as good as you will be tomorrow. You see, gentlemen, we are striving for continued and balanced improvement in this room every single day! If we can accomplish this, then one day you will wake up and you will actually be good!

"Oh, I remember now," recalled Frank. "He used to say that the goal of every practice was to get a little bit better every day. He used to say we would be better than we were yesterday, but not as good as we would be tomorrow, right?"

"That's right Frank," said Al, with approval. "And do you remember what he would say to us at the end of practice, Frank?"

"At the end of practice?" Frank seemed to remember that Coach Ice rarely "said" anything. "Don't you mean what he screamed at us at the end of practice?"

"Yeah, okay, you're right," conceded Al with a chuckle. "Coach Ice rarely spoke in a civil tone as we were doing our wind sprints and circuit training. He screamed at the top of his lungs!"

"And his voice always used to crack!" laughed Frank.

"Remember, no matter how tired we were, we still laughed when his voice would crack!" Al and Frank had quite a laugh recalling Coach Ice and his high-pitched voice cracking. They were having fun reminiscing about the good old days. Nevertheless, while it was good to reminisce and fondly remember those times, Al knew he needed to rally Frank and get back to making him believe in Cornerstone Number Three.

"Yeah...that was funny!" recalled Al. "Do you remember that saying he used to scream at us at the end of practice every day?"

"Something like being good is a stupid idea," recalled Frank.

"Something about competition getting better at a faster rate than you are." "Close," replied Al. "If you want to know exactly what he said at the end of practice every day, just flip over the last card I gave you."

Frank thought to himself, *"No way. There is no way he has what Coach Ice used to say on the back of this card."* Curious, but reluctant, he flipped the card over and saw the following:

"Oh, my gosh! I remember this so clearly now!" said an astonished Frank. "Every single day, he used to scream this out at us — how could I forget?"

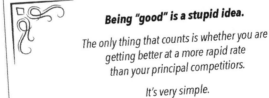

Being "good" is a stupid idea.

The only thing that counts is whether you are getting better at a more rapid rate than your principal competitiors.

It's very simple.

If you are not able to do more, better, faster than they are able to do more, better, faster, then you are getting less-better or more-worse!

"It's okay, Frank, I forgot about it for a while too," acknowledged Al. "I was reading a Tom Peters book three years ago, and lo and behold, this quote is staring me right in the face! I am thinking to myself — Coach didn't make this up! Tom Peters did!"

"Yeah," laughed Frank, "but Coach Ice surely worked it! Tom Peters would have been proud!"

"Yeah, and it was all part of his system for driving continued and balanced improvement. When you look back, Coach Ice developed a system that enabled us to win three national titles during our time there," said Al.

"Yeah, you forget how much impact sports and Coach Ice has had on our lives," Frank added.

Al was sure now that Frank was beginning to make the connection. "What do you mean?" asked Al, trying to draw Frank out.

"Well, let's take the card you just gave me. It's starting to resonate with me that it's not simply 'If at first you don't succeed, try, try again.' Frank went on, "It's more like Coach Ice's practice system of getting a little bit better every single day."

"Really?" Al asked, trying to get Frank to think harder.

"How would you compare and contrast the differences between Coach Ice's system and the old 'if at first you don't succeed' adage?"

"Well," Frank began, "we have to start with the theory of postponed perfection. Ideally, everyone would like to be perfect. But, rather than concentrating on incremental improvement, they continue to put off the opportunity to get a little bit better every day—to progressively improve. Instead, they opt to wait for the final perfection. They don't make the necessary adjustments to improve. Therefore, they are suffering from postponed perfection."

"That's great, Frank!" Al was pleased. "I think you did a great job understanding the front side of the card. Now, why don't you tell me about the back side of the card?"

"The back side?" asked Frank.

"Yes Frank, the back side," Al replied.

"Well, that's easy," Frank said with great confidence. "Put simply, everything in life is in motion. And we are dealing with a highly competitive environment. New graduates are coming off college campuses every day, more educated and more digital than any generation before them. Our competitors can copy our product and service offerings in a matter of months rather than years. With all the knowledge available, via e-learning and the Internet, people and companies can close ranks on any competitive advantage quickly. I recently read about a national research council reporting that it used to take 15 years for 50% of your college education to become obsolete. Do you know what that timeframe is today, Al?"

"No, I don't." replied Al; proud of the way Frank was getting into the discussion.

"It's two years today, Al!" exclaimed Frank. "Two years

for 50% of your college education to become obsolete!"

"So, what you're saying Frank, is that the trick today is not getting an education...it's keeping one, right?"

"You've got it. The trick is to continue to learn so that you can stay competitive because in the grand scheme of things, you are either getting better or worse relative to your competition," replied Frank. He was now focused on the conversation as he started to apply his thoughts to his professional life, wondering why he hadn't done this long ago.

"So, you think that's what the back of the card means — to strive for continued improvement by investing in your own personal development?" asked Al.

"Yes, I do. I think continuing to educate yourself is a big part of it," Frank responded. "But it's more than that. If you think that being good is a stationary place, like a sort of sanctuary, you're sadly mistaken! Going back to what I said earlier — everything in life is in motion. You are either getting better at a more rapid rate than your principal competitors, or they are getting better at a more rapid rate than you. Which, in effect, means you are getting worse!"

"Well said!" Al was proud of his protégée. "I couldn't have said it better myself.

"In a nutshell, "continued Frank, "Progressive improvement means that you must persevere to improve in every aspect of your job — skill, knowledge, preparation, diagnostics, relationship building, etc. That's why it's the third cornerstone. Without the right attitude and the assumption of personal accountability for your actions, successes and failures, Cornerstone Number Three simply will not work."

"That is correct, Frank," confirmed Al. "Does it feel like it is all coming together for you?"

"Absolutely!" Frank responded. "What is the fourth cornerstone?"

Now, pressed for time and the fact that Frank was becoming a quick learner, Al just handed Frank a card that said:

Frank read the card once, then read it again out loud.

"Do you know what that means?" asked Al.

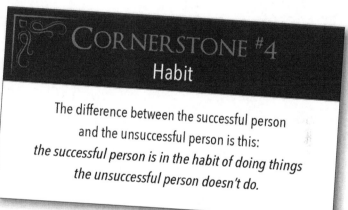

CORNERSTONE #4

Habit

The difference between the successful person and the unsuccessful person is this: the successful person is in the habit of doing things the unsuccessful person doesn't do.

"I think I understand this one, Al." Frank replied as he noticed Al quickly glanced at his watch.

"Why don't you share your thoughts with me. I have time," replied Al.

"It is about doing the right things. It's about creating

positive habits versus negative habits," offered Frank, confidently.

"And as you reflect on the previous three cornerstones, do you understand how they all tie together?" asked Al.

"Yes, I think I do," offered Frank. "I am totally disgusted with all of the bad habits I developed over the past three years. I can't help wondering how this happened to me?"

"Frank, let's not drive the car looking through the rearview mirror. The good news is that you can start developing good habits right here, right now. The way you need to think about the cornerstones is that Attitude and Personal Accountability are about getting your mind right. And Perseverance and Habit are about getting your actions right," explained Al. "Make sense?"

"Yes, it makes perfect sense," confirmed Frank, still wondering to himself how he lost his way.

"Does it feel like a defining moment in your life, Frank?" asked Al.

"More like an epiphany!" exclaimed Frank.

"Well, I am glad we had this quality time together, Frank," as the bartender brought the check. "But it's after eight and I have to be going."

"I'll get it, Al," Frank said reaching for the check. "It's the least I can do for all you have done for me this evening."

"I appreciate that, Frank, but I would like to buy dinner. It's all part of my investment in you — and you need to know, I loved every minute of our time together tonight. How do you feel, Frank?" Al could see that Frank was much more positive than he was when Al arrived at O'Leary's.

"Like I just relieved myself of a mental dump!" Frank laughed.

Al laughed, too, obviously pleased that Frank used the mental dump line he introduced to him earlier that evening.

"That's great, Frank! My job is done! I believe you are now ready to see The Wizard."

"Are you sure, Al? I mean, I had a rough start and a couple of bumps in the road with you tonight, and we are old friends. What makes you think I am ready for The Wizard?"

Al took a moment to consider Frank's question. Truth be told, he was a little worried about the fact he did not go deep enough on the fourth cornerstone. He knew The Wizard had strict criteria for working with Standard's salespeople, which included:

- A President's Roundtable member must sponsor the individual

- The salesperson must have a minimum of two years of sales experience with Standard

- The candidate must also have a complete understanding and acceptance of *The Four Cornerstones of Success*®

- Finally, they must be coming off a recent disappointment and be highly coachable

After a moment of reflection, Al stated with conviction as he began to put on his coat, "Because you now have a clear understanding of *The Four Cornerstones of Success®*, because you are coachable and because I believe in you!"

Al signed for the check.

"Thanks Al. That really means a lot to me. When will this meeting take place?"

Frank was already beginning to worry that he was not worthy enough to meet The Wizard, worrying that he might let his long-time friend and mentor down.

"I am not quite sure yet," responded Al. "I need to get through this Reliant meeting tomorrow, and then I will give you a call to see about your available dates and coordinate those dates with The Wizard."

A very appreciative Frank stood up and extended his hand to thank his long-time friend and mentor.

"Tonight, was great, Al — you have no idea how much I appreciate having you as a friend."

"Yeah, I do," said Al "Right back at you!"

They walked out of O'Leary's and Al quickly hailed a taxicab.

"Remember — nothing's permanent." Al professed. "Not the good times...not the bad times. Trust me; you will bounce back with a vengeance!"

"Yeah, I know. Best of luck with the Reliant presentation tomorrow. I am sure you'll do great!" said Frank as he watched his friend slip into the cab.

Al rolled down the window and responded, "I plan on **becoming the only choice!** As the cab pulled away he shouted, "I'll call you tomorrow!"

"What a great friend," Frank thought to himself. "I can't wait until tomorrow!"

Frank decided to walk home that night in the cool, crisp February air and reflect on the things his good friend and mentor had shared with him. It was only about four or five blocks to his Battery Park apartment, and his mind was racing through *The Four Cornerstones of Success®* over and over again.

Frank thought to himself, *"How could I have let myself backslide so badly with respect to my attitude and personal accountability? Tomorrow will be different."* He made that commitment to himself just as he reached the steps of his building.

Chapter 3: Off to See The Wizard

"The Al Factor"

The next afternoon, Frank headed back to his office after a good day in the field thinking to himself, "I wonder if Al called?"

It was four o'clock and Al should have finished with the Reliant presentation by that time. *"I wonder how he did? He said he was going to become the only choice."* He chuckled aloud as he thought to himself, *"Confidence has never been a problem with Al."*

As he entered the office, Frank stopped by Pam's desk.

Pam was the office administrator and had worked directly with Al while he was in New York. Pam knew about the strong bond between Al and Frank and clearly understood the impact The Wizard had on Al three years earlier.

"Did anyone call?" Frank asked Pam as he walked in the office.

"No, *anyone* didn't call!" snapped a quick-witted Pam in a playful manner.

"No one called?" Frank asked sheepishly. As intense as he was, he didn't catch Pam's playful tone. Pam could see the disappointment on Frank's face, and although she wanted to play the game a little longer, she thought it would be wise — and much kinder — to acquiesce.

"Don't you want to specifically ask if Al called?" asked Pam, knowing the answer to the question.

"Did he?"

"Yes, he did; he called around 2:00 PM," said Pam, matter-of-factly.

"I thought you said no one called!"

"No, I said *anyone* didn't call," chuckled Pam. "Al's not just *anyone* — Al's my main man!"

Pam had always had a special place in her heart for Al. After Al moved to Philadelphia, his positive attitude and leadership was sorely missed by the people in the New York office, and especially by Pam.

As Al started to gain the respect and notoriety that comes with winning contract after contract and achieving the President's Roundtable, Pam, to her credit, coined the term "The Al Factor." Pam firmly believed Standard would never lose a deal in which Al was involved. Many people at the Standard Company agreed with Pam. The term stuck and was used any time Al was hunting a new deal.

"What did he say?" asked Frank. "Did he ask me to call him? How did he do with Reliant?"

"He left you a voice mail," Pam responded.

"Did he say how the presentation with Reliant went?"

"What do you think, Frank?" replied Pam, smiling proudly. "They were dealing with 'The Al Factor'— he became the only choice!"

Frank smiled as he shook his head. "Why doesn't that

surprise me? He told me last night he was going to be the only choice."

"You know what this means?" asked Pam, already knowing the answer.

"What does it mean?" asked Frank .

"This deal will make Al the #1 salesman at Standard and the Director of the President's Roundtable!"

"Wow! I forgot about that!" exclaimed Frank. "That is awesome!"

Just then, Fred Wilson, Frank's manager, walked by and hearing the conversation commented, "I sure hope Al doesn't get a big head over his new title."

Frank immediately came to the rescue of his long-time friend.

"That will never happen to Al. He's the guy that always says, 'Don't get caught reading your own press clippings, because you are never as good as they say you are and you're never as bad as they say you are.' As soon as Al won the deal, I bet you anything he was trying to figure out who else he has in his sales funnel he can use this deal to leverage."

"Well, aren't you going to call him, Frank?" Pam reminded him as Fred moved on.

"Uh, yes" replied Frank. "I am going to call him right now!"

Frank was excited as he listened to Al's voice mail where

Al related an abbreviated version of the Reliant "blow by blow." Frank could not wait to talk to him live on the phone to congratulate him!

"Hello, Al," Frank said when Al answered the phone.

"How you doin' Frank?" asked Al.

"No…how YOU doin'?" said Frank, in his best *Joey Tribiani* imitation.

"I am absolutely great!" replied Al.

"Congratulations on the Reliant deal Al! You are awesome!" Frank exclaimed.

"Thanks, Frank. It was a great win for all of us. It was a total team effort!" replied Al. "Tony, Gail, Larry and Ben all made huge contributions to winning this deal!"

"Yeah, but you were the quarterback, Al," Frank pointed out, mindful of the humility Al had always displayed both as an athlete and as a sales professional.

"You need to give me all the details so that I can emulate your sales prowess!" Frank was beginning to pile it on now. "How does it feel to be the number one top dog at Standard, if you don't mind my asking?"

"I would love to give you all the details, Frank," Al said proudly. "But for you to truly benefit from the details, I think it would be best if we speak after you meet with The Wizard. And all that talk about being number one? Well, I try not to get caught up reading my own press clippings…"

Frank interrupted. "I know, I know — 'because you're never as good as they say you are and you're never as bad as they say you are'— right?"

"That's right, Frank."

"No problem, Al. I'll look forward to the details after I spend time with The Wizard. Speaking of which, were you able to talk with him about me?"

"Yes. I spoke with him earlier this afternoon and shared with him the details of our conversation the other night..."

Frank interrupted again. "Wait, you shared our conversation the other night and he's still willing to meet with me? Wow, you really *can* sell, Al!"

"Frank," Al continued, "we've all been there. That point in our career where we feel like victims. That place where we start to wallow in the 'ain't it awfuls' and the 'woe is me.' Trust me, The Wizard understands that this happens, and although I am not totally positive, I would venture to say he's been there himself. All the great ones have."

"I sure hope you are right," replied Frank. "I'll have to trust you on this."

"And who better to trust than your longtime friend and teammate?" Al responded.

"You've got that right," conceded Frank. "You're always right, though. Now for the big question: Is he willing to meet with me? And if so, when?"

"He has blocked out all day next Wednesday to spend the entire day with you," Al replied. "You will meet with him at his Manhattan apartment at 531 East 81st Street. Be there at 9:00 AM, and don't be late! The Wizard is a stickler on punctuality."

"No problem!" said Frank. "I'm never late! I'll be there."

"Kiss of death." Al quipped.

"What do you mean, 'kiss of death'?" asked Frank.

"Every time someone says something including the word never, the opposite usually happens."

"Well, I hope you're wrong this time, Al," countered Frank.

"I hope so, too. Give me a call after you spend your day with The Wizard and let me know how things went."

"I will, Al. And thanks for arranging this meeting. Do I need to bring anything?'

"Just bring an open mind and a thirst to learn from the best I have ever seen. That is all you need to bring," said Al, fondly remembering his first day with The Wizard.

"Will do," replied Frank.

They said good-bye and hung up the phone.

Frank got nervous butterflies in his stomach as he thought about the upcoming meeting. He had less than six days to get in the right frame of mind to meet with The Wizard. The excitement of the meeting gave Frank trouble sleeping the first couple of nights. He wondered if he was worthy. He wondered if he was ready. He wondered if he would be able to make the necessary adjustments and would be as successful as Al. He wondered about a lot of things...

Wednesday with The Wizard

It's 8:50 AM, and Frank is in a taxicab stuck in traffic, wondering why he took a cab in the first place. Wondering why he didn't take the subway. Wondering why he had used the word never! He was coming to grips with the fact that regardless of what he did at this point, he would be at least ten minutes late. He considered jumping out of the cab and making a dash for it. Then, picturing himself meeting The Wizard dripping with sweat, he quickly decided that would not be in his best interest. He thought to call the Wizard and realized he didn't have his number. He decided to call Al and got his voice mail.

"What to do next?" he thought to himself. *"I'll call Pam; maybe she has his number!"* As the clock struck 9:00 AM, he hung up the phone with Pam with yet another unsuccessful attempt at trying to get The Wizard's telephone number. Just then, traffic started to move.

"I am sooo going to be late!" Frank said to himself as he gazed out the window and his anxiety reached a fever pitch.

"Al was right. I should never say never; it's the kiss of death."

Finally, the taxicab pulled up in front of The Wizard's building. It was 9:10 AM. The fare was $14.60. Frank handed the driver a twenty and said, "Keep the change!" as he hustled himself out of the cab and up the stairs to the entrance of the building.

When he arrived at The Wizard's apartment, he felt the butterflies in his stomach again and his body was tensed with fear. He knew how important this meeting was, and he wanted to make the best possible impression on The Wizard.

"What am I going to say to this man?" Frank asked himself. *"How am I going to justify being twelve minutes late to a guy who is a stickler for punctuality?"*

He glanced down at his watch, which now read 9:12.

"Wait a minute," he thought, *"he lives in New York. He'll understand the situation with the traffic."* He started to knock on the door, then pulled back and thought to himself, *"What if he doesn't? What am I going to say... What am I going to say?"*

Just then, the door swung open and a man peered out, asking, "Are you Frank Kelly?"

"Uh, yes, I am," Frank replied, both awestruck and embarrassed for being late.

"Hi, I am Jack Anderson. Come on in. I have been expecting you."

"Nice to finally meet you," replied Frank as he entered the apartment.

Frank looked at Jack Anderson, the man known as The Wizard, as he followed him into his home. The Wizard was not a very big man. He was probably a good three to four inches shorter than Frank's five-foot, ten-inch frame. It was readily apparent that Jack was quite physically fit for a man of any age, not to mention for a man of 55 years. Frank marveled at his broad shoulders and small waist.

"This man cannot be fifty-five years old," Frank thought to himself as he followed him down the hall. Though his hair was grey and slightly thinning, he did not look a day over forty-five.

"I am very sorry I am late," Frank stammered. "I was stuck in traffic. Like that is a real surprise to you, living in New York." Frank hoped he could get The Wizard to buy into his somewhat lame excuse.

"Yes, the traffic can be tough," acknowledged The Wizard.

For a moment, it appeared he was going to let Frank off the hook for his twelve-minute tardiness. But then he shifted gears as he turned to look directly at Frank. His piercing blue eyes looked right into Frank's.

"Frank, let me ask you a question. Do you know how long a person can go without oxygen?"

"I beg your pardon, sir?" Frank was clearly confused by this unexpected question and was becoming uncomfortable as he felt The Wizard look right into his very soul.

"Do you know how long a person can go without oxygen?"

"Uh, uh...oh...I don't know," stammered Frank. "Maybe three to five minutes?"

"Five minutes is about it. Thank God, I wasn't waiting for you to deliver oxygen because I would be dead right now!" responded The Wizard.

He had Frank's full attention now.

"Do you understand what I mean?" he asked, with those piercing blue eyes looking intently at Frank

"Yes, sir," responded Frank. There was no question that he was being held accountable for being twelve minutes late — and with a lame excuse, to boot.

"I am sorry and it will *never* happen again." Frank immediately regretted his use of the word "never"; it just came out of his mouth before he could get it back.

"Never say never!" The Wizard responded.

Frank interrupted before he could finish his thought. "I know, it's the kiss of death."

"Right. I personally try to never say never," acknowledged The Wizard as he led Frank into a room that appeared to be a rather large study with bookshelves crammed with memorabilia covering the remaining wall space.

"Have a seat and make yourself comfortable."

He motioned to Frank to sit in one of the large leather

chairs opposite Jack with only a mahogany coffee table in between them. As Frank sat down, he felt compelled to share with The Wizard what went wrong this morning, causing him to be late.

"You know, Mr. Anderson, things started out okay this morning, and I thought I had plenty of time until I hit First Avenue coming uptown," Frank said as he started to justify being late.

"Frank," The Wizard interrupted. "Do you know the difference between the successful salesperson and the unsuccessful salesperson?"

"Um…I am not sure."

Frank knew he had not made the best impression and was not willing to stick his neck out any further at this point.

The Wizard handed Frank a card:

Frank read the card once to himself, and then slowly read the card again, realizing that he had seen this card before.

As he was reading the card a third time to himself, The Wizard asked, "Do you know what that card means?"

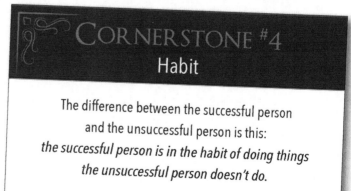

CORNERSTONE #4
Habit

The difference between the successful person and the unsuccessful person is this: the successful person is in the habit of doing things the unsuccessful person doesn't do.

"Yes," said Frank, sheepishly.

"Why don't you explain it to me, if you don't mind."

"Well, Al shared this with me right before we wrapped up our talk together. I think it means that there are good habits and bad habits, right?"

"Go on," said The Wizard.

"Well, I guess the successful salesperson has mastered good habits, and the inverse of that is that the unsuccessful salesperson has not," Frank shared thoughtfully.

"That is certainly one way to put it," said The Wizard. "Why don't you give me an example?"

"It could be one of a lot of things…like showing up to meetings on time," Frank confessed.

"That would certainly be considered a good habit. Why do you think people show up late for meetings, Frank?"

"There are probably a number of reasons." Frank was beginning to feel uncomfortable. "It could be poor planning, or perhaps it was something that was out of the person's control."

"Like traffic? Traffic is not in your control, is it Frank?"

"Yes, like traffic. You never know what you are going to get when you're in Manhattan."

"Is this your first time in Manhattan, Frank?" asked The Wizard. He obviously already knew the answer to the question.

"No. I work here every day. The Financial District is

my territory."

"So you work here every day," confirmed The Wizard scratching his chin as he thought of the next question to ask. "Do you ever ride the subways Frank?"

"Yes," Frank was beginning to sense where the conversation was going. "I ride the subways every day."

"Then you must know that the way to offset New York City traffic is to ride the subways," stated The Wizard. "They are 98% on time. Are you 98% on time for meetings, Frank?"

"No," confessed Frank, "probably closer to 90%."

"Frank," The Wizard continued, as he began setting the tone for the day, "I was assured by Al that you had a complete understanding of the four cornerstones..."

Frank interrupted, "I do, Mr. Anderson," feeling like a grade school boy being lectured for coming late to class. "I completely buy into *The Four Cornerstones of Success*® consisting of Attitude, Personal Accountability, Perseverance and Habit."

"You do?" The Wizard asked with a bewildered look.

"I do, absolutely." Beads of sweat began to form on Frank's forehead.

"Well, then, I trust I won't have to hear any more lame excuses from you," snapped The Wizard. "Because when we accept personal accountability for our actions, one would clearly understand that a poor choice was made in taking a taxi rather than taking the subway; isn't that right, Frank? And please call me Jack. There are no formalities around here."

"No formalities around here," Frank thought to himself. *"Here I am, a grown man getting a tongue lashing, and this guy tells me there are no formalities around here."*

"Yes sir — I mean, Jack" replied Frank awkwardly. "I get the point. It's about being in the habit of planning better and being in the habit of accepting personal accountability for my actions. Trust me. I do understand."

"Successful habits are the keys to a successful salesperson," offered The Wizard. "Good habits are like pillars of strength and optimism. They keep you focused and disciplined. They help you do the right things. Bad habits are like shackles that both slow you down and tear you down link by link. Bad habits are like comfortable beds...easy to get into and difficult to get out of."

Frank remembered how he had heard a similar description about bad habits from Al when they had dinner together. He thought to himself, *"So that's where Al gets this stuff."*

 The Wizard continued, "You were a former athlete, Frank. How did bad habits serve you in wrestling?"

"Not very well," replied Frank, as he thought about the question. "They caused a lot more losses than wins, I guess."

"Bad habits serve you the same way in sales and in business," said The Wizard. "What I am going to share with you today are a number of good habits and good approaches to business. We're going to talk about active listening, being in the customer's operating reality, understanding their buying/decision process, objection handling and relationship management. If you do not work to get a little bit better every day and make good habits part of your daily routine, you will continue to struggle; understand?"

"Understood." Frank was beginning to look forward to understanding the approach and methodology The Wizard was going to share with him.

"Good," said The Wizard. "Right now, I would like to take the time to learn a little more about you. Can you tell me a little bit about yourself, Frank?"

"Sure," said Frank. "Where would you like me to begin?"

"At the beginning, if it's all right with you."

"Okay, the beginning it is. I am one of seven children, born in New York City, and my parents' names are Bill and Ellen Kelly."

"What number are you in the birth order, Frank?"

"Number four. I have one sister older and one sister younger. I have two brothers older and two brothers younger."

"That makes you the middle child, correct?"

"That's correct, sir," replied Frank.

"Please, Frank, call me Jack," The Wizard said, seeming

to soften his tone. "As I said before, there are no formalities around here."

Frank could see by the sincerity on The Wizard's face that he was genuinely interested in learning more about him.

Frank went on to share all the details of his life — his relationship with his parents and siblings, his favorite subjects in school, the sports he played in high school, the college he graduated from and why he chose that school. They even discussed what year he graduated, why he chose to wrestle in college, why he chose Standard as his employer and how much influence Al had on that decision.

It was by no means, a one-way conversation. The Wizard asked Frank clarifying and exploratory questions all along the way. He asked Frank what he felt he did well and where he felt he needed to improve.

As the conversation progressed, Frank opened-up to The Wizard and did not hold back. The conversation was cordial and there was a good exchange of information. Frank looked at his watch, noticing it was almost 10:00 AM and realized he had spent most of the past forty-five minutes talking about himself.

"How am I going to get the knowledge from The Wizard if I keep talking about me," Frank thought to himself.

Against his better judgment and for purely selfish reasons, Frank decided to intervene and ask The Wizard a question to get back on what he saw as the learning path.

"Jack," Frank interrupted. "I beg your pardon, but I just spent the last forty-five minutes talking about me, and I was under the impression I had come here to learn from the great Jack Anderson. When does the lesson start?"

"Right now."

The Wizard reached into his pocket and handed Frank a card: Frank took the card from The Wizard.

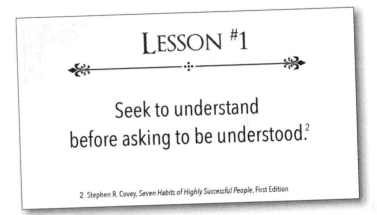

LESSON #1

Seek to understand
before asking to be understood.[2]

2. Stephen R. Covey, *Seven Habits of Highly Successful People*, First Edition

Reading the card, he thought to himself, *"What an idiot I am! Here he was trying to understand more about me, assess my strengths and weaknesses, and I go totally on the offensive! I wouldn't blame him if he asked me to leave!"*

"Do you understand what the card means, Frank?"

"I think so," Frank responded deliberately. "It means to invest time in the people and understand them before you start asking them to understand you."

"That's good. The most important thing we can do in any relationship is to take the time to listen. It shows our investment in the other person and that their needs and wants are more important to us than our own. This is one of the greatest relationship builders there is. Do you think this would be a valuable approach with customers?"

"Yes. It makes perfect sense to me," said Frank. "I guess that's why you took the time to get to know me better before you asked me to understand you. The same principle applies with customers."

"That's exactly right, Frank. Listening is the most flattering thing you can do with another person. Because you are in effect saying, your thoughts are more important than mine."

The Wizard continued, "God gave us two ears and one mouth. That's why we should be doing twice as much listening as talking. Let me ask you a question: when was the last time you learned something while speaking?"

Frank smiled at the two ears and one mouth analogy.

As he listened and thought about the question for a moment, he responded, "Probably never. I guess it would be virtually impossible to learn while you are speaking!"

"As far back as I can remember," The Wizard continued, "I don't believe I have ever learned anything while I was flapping my gums."

The Wizard obviously took great pride in his listening skills. He had an incredible knack for getting people to open-up and share information with him, whether it was listening to a customer brag about his or her thirteen-year-old playing on a travel team or sharing confidential information about a company reorganization. He had learned a long time ago that there is a big difference between just listening and listening to truly understand what was being said, or active listening.

Frank confessed, "I am sure I could get lots better at listening."

"But, keep in mind that it's one thing to get better at listening, and it's quite another to master active listening," proclaimed The Wizard.

"Active listening?" Frank was not familiar with the term.

"Active listening," repeated The Wizard. "That is listening to understand rather than listening to merely hear."

Frank had a puzzled look on his face. "What's the difference?" he thought to himself.

"You're not familiar with the difference between listening and active listening, Frank?" asked The Wizard, noticing that Frank was struggling with the new term.

"Not really," confessed Frank.

"Well, then, the best way I can help you to understand is by playing a quick game to test your listening skills. Are you up for a quick game?"

"I guess so," Frank responded cautiously, seeing the look on The Wizard's face when he mentioned playing a game.

"Okay, Frank, you need to listen carefully and answer quickly," instructed The Wizard.

"Say silk five times fast!"

"Silk, silk, silk, silk, silk!" Frank responded quickly.

"What do cows drink?" asked The Wizard. "Quickly!"

Frank responded as fast as he could, "Milk!"

"No, Frank, cows don't drink milk, they give milk!" countered The Wizard, knowing he just made his point.

"You heard the question, Frank, you just didn't listen to understand the question."

"Point well taken!" Frank grudgingly admitted. He chuckled at the quick little exercise The Wizard had used to make his point — and it did clearly make the point.

"Where did you get that great little exercise?"

"From my granddaughter, Keely." The Wizard was struggling to hold back his laughter.

"I obviously need help if your granddaughter duped me!" admitted Frank.

"You would be surprised how many people I catch with that test," said The Wizard. "Most people hear, but don't actively listen, or listen to understand. A great example is how many times people forget a person's name after being introduced to them only moments before."

"That happens to me a lot," confessed Frank, wondering if he should have made that small confession so soon in the process.

"If you make the person you are being introduced to the most important person in the room at the time of introduction, you won't have that problem," explained The Wizard. "It is a fairly simple technique."

The Wizard took the time to explain to Frank the

importance of active listening. He shared with Frank that most people can tell when someone is really listening to understand versus just going through the motions.

 Through the process, Frank was beginning to gain an understanding of the importance of active listening in building relationships.

"So, Frank, tell me about one of the sales calls you had yesterday," said The Wizard, shifting gears. "One of the better ones."

"Well, I had a good call with the buyer at the Wheeler company yesterday," Frank said.

"So what happened?" asked The Wizard.

"As I entered his office, I scanned the place for some common ground we could talk about and saw his degree hanging on the wall. I noticed that he graduated from the same college as my brother, Bill. We had a good conversation about the 'good ole days,' and I think we built good rapport right out of the chute. Then I was able to pitch him on our total cost reduction program, and he seemed very interested."

"What happened after you made your pitch?" The Wizard had a feeling he already knew the answer to the question.

"Well, he said he had to cut the meeting short because he had another meeting," Frank admitted reluctantly, feeling the pressure to add something positive.

"However, he asked me to give him a call next month so that we could pick up where we left off."

"And you did say that was a good sales call, right?" asked The Wizard.

"Yes," confirmed Frank.

"Why?"

"Because I closed for another meeting and he said he would meet with me."

Frank was feeling a little defensive.

"You said you closed for another meeting," recounted The Wizard. "When is it scheduled for?"

"Well, it is not actually scheduled yet," Frank admitted. "Like I said, he said to call him next month."

"I see." The Wizard shifted gears again. "Did he like the Total Cost Reduction program you pitched?"

"Well, I think so. He didn't express any major objections," responded Frank.

"He didn't express any major objections, you say? What problems was he experiencing that this program would help him with?" asked The Wizard.

"Problems?"

"Yes. Where is his pain?" asked The Wizard.

"Obviously, Frank, things weren't perfect at Wheeler. He wouldn't spend time with you if he felt everything was perfect."

Frank sat up in his chair and began his own version of listening to understand. The Wizard did make a valid point and Frank, quite honestly, didn't know the answer to the question.

"So where was his pain?" The Wizard asked again.

He was not letting up even though he could see Frank was seriously pondering the question.

After considering the question one more time, Frank reluctantly admitted, "I am sorry to say, I don't know."

"You did say that you went into a sales pitch on a Total Cost Reduction Program," recalled The Wizard. "Why would you do that without understanding what his problems were?"

"Because it is my experience that everyone wants to reduce costs. Chances are, Wheeler is no different."

"Maybe. But suppose his current supplier won the original contract with a low bid and he is suffering from quality issues that are not effectively tracked under a cost reduction program?" asked The Wizard.

"How effective do you think your sales pitch was on Total Cost Reduction if that were the case?"

Frank gave it some thought before responding, "Probably not very. But how do you know he wasn't looking for a Total Cost Reduction Program?"

"I honestly don't know Frank, but neither do you," replied The Wizard. "Do me a favor and turn over the card I just gave you and read the back."

Frank turned the card over and read:

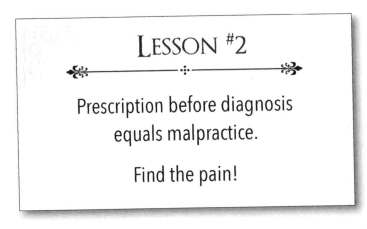

LESSON #2

Prescription before diagnosis
equals malpractice.

Find the pain!

As Frank was absorbing what he had just read, The Wizard continued with the lesson.

"How would you like to go to the doctor feeling very ill and have him prescribe drugs for you without asking you any questions or doing any diagnostics?"

Frank replied, "I wouldn't feel very confident in the doctor if he didn't take the time to ask me questions and understand what was bothering me."

"Exactly!" agreed The Wizard. "Yet all over the world, every minute of every day, there is a salesperson going into a sales pitch with a potential customer without ever taking the time to understand where the *GAP* is."

"GAP? What do you mean by *GAP*, Jack?"

"*GAP*, put simply, is the difference between the customer's desired state and his or her actual state," responded The Wizard. "It is something I was taught many years ago by a very talented salesperson — coincidentally named Jack — and it looks like this."

The Wizard picked up a remote control off the mahogany coffee table sitting between them, and he walked over to the beautifully sculpted mahogany woodwork on the walls. The walls began to open revealing a whiteboard.

After speaking with The Wizard for a little over an hour and then watching the walls open automatically as he pressed the remote control, Frank could easily understand where he got his nickname. The Wizard picked up a dry erase marker and began to draw on the board:

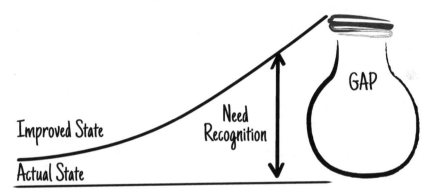

The Wizard then proceeded to ask Frank if he understood what he had just written on the board.

Frank responded, "I believe the goal is to understand if there is a gap between what the customer would like versus what the customer is actually receiving. It appears that if you can create GAP, you create an area of opportunity for you to fill that GAP."

"Is that what you mean by finding the pain?" asked Frank.

"Yes, Frank, you nailed it right on the head!" offered an enthused The Wizard.

"Like with the doctor's example, if we as professional sales people start pitching a solution before we know what the problem is, then we are creating our own version of malpractice which yields a lack of trust from our customers."

"I understand your point, Jack. But I came to Standard because they had a good sales training program. One of the things they emphasized is the importance of the relationship. I haven't heard you speak of relationship once in our first hour and a half together. Do you think there is no need for rapport and/or relationship? Or do you believe that purely finding the pain is the way to go?"

"That's a fair question," acknowledged The Wizard. "It is not a case of either/or; it's a more a case of both/and."

"Huh?" responded Frank, looking confused.

"Relationship and where you are in the relationship play a significant role in successful selling. I plan on addressing this in greater detail later. But for now, let's talk about that sales call yesterday with Wheeler Company while you were in your rapport-building mode. What exactly did you do?"

"Well, as I walked into his office, I saw his degree hanging on his wall and asked him how he liked college." Frank replied. "I asked him why he chose that school, and after he told me why, it was coincidently the same reason my brother Bill chose the same school. He asked me what years my brother had attended, and I answered him. I asked him if the Thursday nights at The Pub were as fun and crowded as my brother used to say they were. We talked about things like that."

"Do you remember the Lesson #1 card and what it said?" asked The Wizard.

"Of course, I have it right here. 'Seek to understand before asking to be understood.'" Frank thought about what he had just told The Wizard about his relationship building and how he asked the gentleman from Wheeler several questions that showed that he was genuinely interested in him as a person.

"Do you feel that you exemplified what is on the card?' asked The Wizard.

"I guess I did on the rapport-building side," said Frank. "And then I guess I blew it when I went into a Total Cost Reduction sales pitch."

"And how do you think that the Total Cost Reduction sales pitch affected the outcome of the meeting?" asked The Wizard.

"Well, he listened while I did all the talking. He had virtually no questions or objections," Frank recalled. "And then he cut the meeting short and told me to call him in a month."

As The Wizard sat back in his chair, Frank thought to himself, putting two and two together, *"Oh, brother! The Wizard must think I am a total loser because I told him that was one of my better sales calls! He must be imagining what one of my bad sales calls looks like!"*

"And do you believe you made any effort to uncover the *GAP* or find the pain?"

"I think we both now know the answer to that question," replied a discouraged and embarrassed Frank. "No, I didn't have a clue."

"A sort of prescription before diagnosis, right, Frank?"

"Obviously." Frank was feeling worse by the minute and wondering what The Wizard thought of him. He wondered if he would survive the day without being sent home early. In his brief time with The Wizard he had...

1. Arrived late

2. Failed to accept personal accountability for arriving late

3. Failed a test on active listening

4. Shared a disaster of a sales call with him that he actually labeled as a good sales call

"This guy must think I am a total loser," Frank thought to himself.

Becoming a Trusted Advisor

The Wizard, seeing that he had made his point and noticing the deflated look on Frank's face, decided to move the conversation to a different topic by eliciting Frank's goals with respect to his customer relationships.

"Frank, what type of relationship do you want with your

customers?" asked The Wizard curiously.

Frank thought about The Wizard's question for a moment before saying, "Well, I guess I want the type of relationship where the customer likes me and counts on me to deliver. I want them to trust me… to know that I will do what I say, and to see me as a solutions provider rather than as a vendor."

"You deliver on what you say you will, they trust you, and you provide solutions to help them with their problems. Do I have that right?"

"Yes. That would work for me," replied Frank.

"A sort of Trusted Advisor, then?" offered The Wizard, realizing this would be a new concept for Frank.

"Trusted Advisor," Frank said, as he processed the new term. "Trusted Advisor — yes, I like that a lot."

"Good. One of my dearest customers referred to me as a Trusted Advisor nearly twenty-seven years ago," The Wizard said. "And that is the minimum I would accept in any relationship with my customers."

"I like that — a Trusted Advisor," acknowledged Frank.

The change of topic seemed to take the pressure off a little bit.

"Did you ever ask him why he used that term to describe you?"

"Yes, of course." answered The Wizard. "He said that I had empathy and subject matter expertise, and that I always looked at problems as though I were looking at them through his eyes. This very dear customer also introduced me to the term Operating Reality.

"Operating reality?" asked Frank. Two new terms in less than a minute! *What did he mean by the term operating reality?"*

"Operating reality is a key term for our learning today. Being in a customer's operating reality means ***being able to see problems and opportunities as they appear through the customer or prospect's eyes***. It is your ability to help them:

1. Solve current problems

2. Prevent future problems

3. Increase efficiency & effectiveness

4. Increase productivity

5. Reduce day to day friction

6. Meet deadlines

7. Maintain a sense of well being

Being in a customer's operating reality means you see problems and opportunities as they exist in the eyes of the customer," The Wizard explained patiently.

"Do you mean having empathy?" offered Frank, trying to translate the term into a simpler context.

"Yes, empathy is certainly a part of it. But it's more like empathy on steroids. It is truly the ability to perceive problems and opportunities through the eyes of the customer and make a concerted effort to help that customer improve business performance in line with his or her personal and or business objectives."[5]

"Let's take you as an example, Frank. Whose operating reality were you in when you launched into the Total Cost Reduction sales pitch with your contact from Wheeler?"

"Clearly, I was living in my own operating reality," responded Frank. The picture suddenly crystallized right before his eyes.

"Great sales professionals are masters of active listening, and they do so in the customer's operating reality," declared The Wizard, as he handed Frank a card labeled Lesson #3:

"Something to aspire to for sure," offered Frank. He was beginning to realize how difficult the task would actually be.

LESSON #3

A trusted advisor is always in the **customer's** operating reality.

"Aspire to?" asked The Wizard.

He was hoping that use of the word "aspire" reflected Frank's commitment and dedication to continued and balanced improvement.

"Yeah, well, I mean, I don't think the type of change we are talking about here will happen overnight," offered Frank. "But I am committed to progressive improvement!"

 "Good!" said The Wizard. "Well, Frank, It's close to 10:45 AM and we should probably take a break. Let's start back up at 11:00 AM. But before we do that, why don't you summarize on the whiteboard what you have learned so far, in your own words."

"Including the four cornerstones, Jack?" asked Frank.

"Yes."

With that, The Wizard left the room to let Frank complete the assigned task.

Frank picked up a marker and wrote:

Frank's Key Learnings:

1. Attitude is the start of everything
2. Personal accountability — look in the mirror first
3. Perseverance — I must strive for progressive improvement, faster than my competition
4. Habits: I must develop good habits and eliminate bad habits
5. Listen — I must seek to understand before asking to be understood
6. Prescription before diagnosis equals malpractice

7. Operating Reality: I must be in the customer's operating reality in order to truly find the pain.

Creating Value for Your Customers

After reading what he had written, Frank felt comfortable that he had a clear understanding of the importance of each of the points.

As Frank waited for The Wizard to return to the room, he marveled at all of the wisdom he had learned this morning. And he was amazed at the memorabilia on the walls. As a salesperson, The Wizard had been a member of the President's Roundtable eighteen years in a row.

Even more incredibly, he was the Director for his final twelve years in sales before being promoted into sales management. Frank had heard that The Wizard resisted sales management for a long time due to his commitment to his long-time and very loyal customers. He had also heard it said at Standard that The Wizard was the first to develop a Customer First, Customer for Life™ Philosophy whereby he never lost a customer.

As a sales manager, The Wizard was sent all over the country — New York, Chicago, Los Angeles, Atlanta and Philadelphia. Each of these districts was a problem area when he arrived, and now they were among the top ten districts in the United States for Standard. The Wizard had not only made his mark as a phenomenal salesperson, but he was an even stronger sales leader. As Frank read some of the inspirational statements posted on the wall, he could remember having heard the same words from Al less than a week before. Almost as impressive as the contents of the wall was the vast number of books on the shelves of the study. Frank wondered if The Wizard had read them all.

Just as he wondered, The Wizard returned, asking Frank if he had any questions.

"It's a little off the subject, but if you don't mind me asking, how many of these books have you actually read?" asked Frank.

"I don't mind the question," replied The Wizard. "I have read every one of them."

"Every one of them?" Frank was amazed. "There must be at least 500 books on those shelves!"

"Easily," said The Wizard. "More likely it's closer to 600."

"How did you ever find the time to read all those books?" asked Frank.

"Thirty minutes a day, Frank, five days a week. I invest at least that much time in my self-development by reading something related to my profession or related to my customers' business," explained The Wizard. "I made a commitment to myself that I would be a student of the game. That is, that I would persevere in the spirit of progressive improvement. When you live up to a commitment to yourself like that, thirty years later you find you have nearly 600 books in your study."

"Wow, I guess this is the ultimate example of progressive improvement!" Frank was in awe of the man sitting across from him and no longer had any doubt about why he was called The Wizard.

"And you actually kept track of this?"

"Yes, I do," replied The Wizard. "I recorded each book that I read in a ledger to start out with, and now on my computer. You see, Frank, it's one thing to say you are going to strive to get a little bit better every day, and it's quite another to actually make the effort to keep track of your own personal development over all of those years."

He pointed to one of the inspirational sayings hanging on his wall:

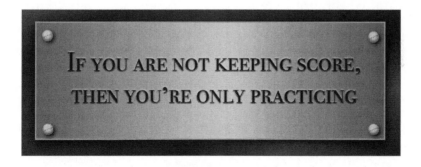

IF YOU ARE NOT KEEPING SCORE,
THEN YOU'RE ONLY PRACTICING

"I saw that," said Frank. "It reminds me of something my old college coach would have said."

"Coach Ice?" asked The Wizard. "He is a man after my own heart!"

"You **know** him?" asked Frank.

He was wondering how The Wizard could possibly have met his former college coach.

"I know of him," replied The Wizard. "Al speaks about him and his teachings quite often. I like his style. And five national championships to his credit are a testament to his commitment to his team and to the sport. I am sure he was the type of coach that kept score."

"Yes, he has quite a track record." Frank was proud of the fact that he had had the opportunity to compete for Coach Ice.

"You said before, Jack, that you were 'a student of the game.' What did you mean by that?"

"Much like you were probably a student of the game in college during your time on the wrestling team, I am a student of the game as it relates to business. The name of the game is consultative selling — and the end game is value creation on behalf of my customers," explained The Wizard.

"Now, I know that *value creation* is a fancy buzzword and it is often overused. But success in your career truly starts with your understanding of what business you are in. You see, Frank, I am in the *customer business*, first and foremost."

"Consultative selling." The term was familiar to Frank. Standard used the term in its training material. "I understand that, but value creation? What do you mean by value creation?"

"Consultative selling is what you see if you are in your operating reality," explained The Wizard. "Value creation is the output that benefits your customers as a result of a consultative selling effort. We all are customers at one time or another and before making a purchase decision will go through a very simple equation in our mind." The Wizard walked over to the whiteboard, and wrote the following below Frank's Lessons Learned:

$$\text{Value} = \text{Benefits} - \text{Cost}$$

He continued, "You see, Frank, in this equation the benefits should always outweigh the cost in order to create value for the customer."

"I see," Frank said slowly. He was beginning to understand the logic. "Does that principle ever conflict with what you did while selling for Standard?"

"I'm not sure I understand your question," said The Wizard, puzzled.

"Well," Frank started, choosing his words carefully, "being a commissioned salesperson, did you ever put more value on what you were selling in terms of your commission than you did on creating value for your customer?"

Frank continued, as it became clear The Wizard wasn't quite sure where he was going. "Standard wanted you to sell more to your customers and customers — at least the ones I have been selling to — typically want to buy as little as possible. So, weren't you ever inclined to try to sell them more than they actually needed, for your own benefit and Standard's sake?"

"No, not at all Frank," responded The Wizard.

"True, Standard wanted me to grow my business. However, nowhere in any training I received from the company did they ever tell me to sell customers more than they needed to buy.

My job was to create value for my customers by helping them meet their needs and solve their business problems. From my perspective, it really didn't matter how much I sold them as long as it resulted in improved business performance for my customers and retaining my position with them as a Trusted Advisor."

"Didn't you ever want to go for the 'quick hit'?" Frank persisted. He was somewhat uncomfortable with the line of questioning he had begun, but he needed to ask for his own benefit.

"The quick hit? Never, Frank," declared The Wizard. "I always treated customer relationships like running a marathon around a track. I am in it for the long haul and know I will be coming back around to see that customer on a regular basis. In some cases, I sold some customers less than I did in the prior year for a variety of reasons. By not overselling and by making a conscious effort to stay in their operating reality, they knew I was in the relationship for the long haul. Therefore, I knew I could count on any one of them as a strong reference for new business."

"That's a good way of looking at things. You were obviously very successful. I mean, how many managers are nicknamed The Wizard by their people?"

"Yeah, yeah, yeah," muttered The Wizard, clearly embarrassed by the nickname. "Let's just make sure you call me Jack!"

"No problem, Jack. Can I ask how you were you able to stay so focused on creating value for your customers all those years even with a quota breathing down your neck?"

"Good question. We are now at the point in our discussion where it is important to understand a little bit about the combination of operating reality, process management and relationship management," responded The Wizard.

"It's 11:45AM now. Let's break for lunch and pick up the lesson again at 1:00 PM. We could take a walk to the corner deli and grab a bite, if you'd like. I am curious to learn more about who Frank Kelly really is and what makes him tick."

"That would be 'seeking to understand...'right, Jack?" Frank was proud of his grasp of the day's lessons.

"Sort of. Or it could be a way for me to get a great New York Reuben sandwich for lunch!" joked The Wizard.

They both had a good chuckle as they put on their

coats and headed out the door. At lunch, Frank learned much more about The Wizard than he had hoped for. The Wizard was a former Marine, ex-Vietnam combat veteran, and had been awarded the Purple Heart. The Purple Heart is awarded to members of the armed forces who are wounded by an instrument of war at the hands of the enemy. The Wizard still had the seven-inch scar on his left inner thigh where the shrapnel from the enemy grenade landed, cutting his combat duty short.

During his nearly thirty years at Standard, The Wizard had established himself as the best sales professional in Standard's history. He spent the first twenty years of his Standard career in sales building his customer base to unprecedented levels, and the last ten years in sales management teaching those who were willing to learn from him how to be the best.

Frank, who had been very curious about the nickname, finally asked The Wizard where it had come from. This forced The Wizard into an uncomfortable zone — talking about his successful sales career. It was becoming clear to Frank that humility was one of The Wizard's biggest traits.

As the story goes, The Wizard related, he earned his nickname while in Chicago working with an up and coming National Account Manager named Mary Ann Panlin. The Wizard was helping Mary Ann transition from a successful sales career to the more strategic role of a National Account Manager, selling multi-million-dollar contracts to the C-Level. Teaching Mary Ann about the basics in creating value for the customers, he informed Mary Ann that the thing that most commonly prevents sales people from winning the business isn't what they know — it's what they don't know.

He shared a structured, repeatable methodology to gain insight into the needs and wants of the customer. How to ask the tough questions in a softer way to gain insight into:

1. Who the Key Decision Maker is?

2. Who the Key Decision influencers are?

3. What their critical concerns and objectives are as it relates to Standard's products and services?

4. How this project fits their hierarchy?

5. What's the decision process?

6. What's the decision criteria?

7. Understanding the political landscape

He then showed Mary Ann what a good sales call looked like and began to teach her how to help customers understand their needs in a new or different way, using a specific set of questions to gain information and insight into the customer's operating reality.

After winning a much-coveted contract using his process, Mary Ann dubbed Jack "The Wizard — the man who sees all and knows all!" And so the name stuck.

Focus to Win

As the two men returned to the apartment after lunch, each took the time to check voicemail.

Frank had received two messages during lunch and handled both of them relatively quickly. The Wizard, meanwhile, was on the phone quite a bit longer, talking sales strategy with one of Standard's top sales people, ironically the same Mary Ann Panlin that had given Jack Anderson the nickname The Wizard.

Frank couldn't help but overhear some of the conversation.

"Let's make sure we have a clear understanding of the decision criteria and the decision process, Mary Ann," said The Wizard just before he ended the call.

"Do you still have a lot of conversations with Standard sales people?" asked Frank.

"Well, I spoke with Al yesterday, Mary Ann today — and you're here, aren't you?" replied The Wizard.

"I take that to be a yes," said Frank, realizing he had asked a question with an obvious answer.

"Correct." responded the Wizard. "Now, let's get back to work."

He walked over to the whiteboard and began to write, adding to Frank's list of lessons learned:

8. The Buying/Decision Process and Creating the Identification of Need

9. Effective use of the Call Planning Worksheet

10. The SIGN effective questions

11. Objection handling — LAER

12. Merging the Sales and Buying/Decision Process

13. The Relationship Pyramid

"Building off The Four Cornerstones of Success® Al shared with you," began The Wizard, "and the lessons we discussed this morning, there are six additional topics we need to cover that will help position you to become the only choice."

"Become the only choice..." Frank thought to himself. *"That's the line Al uses. It is easy to see where Al got some of his wisdom and expertise."*

"Can you begin to see the logic — a sort of set of pearls we are stringing together?" asked The Wizard.

"I think so," replied Frank.

"Why don't you explain it to me," asked The Wizard, testing for understanding."

"Okay," said Frank, pausing to put his thoughts together. He was much more comfortable now with The Wizard and didn't feel nearly as threatened as he did when he showed up on his doorstep, late. "The first three cornerstones were about character. With Attitude, it is the ability to find the positives and the opportunities in every situation. Second, I need to hold myself accountable for my results and third, I need to make sure I persevere by making an effort to get a little bit better every single day."

"And the fourth cornerstone, Frank?"

"Developing good habits are the key to success," responded Frank. "Bad habits are like comfortable beds, easy to get into and difficult to get out of. It's kind of like that wisdom statement you have hanging on your wall," offered Frank as he pointed to the framed photo:

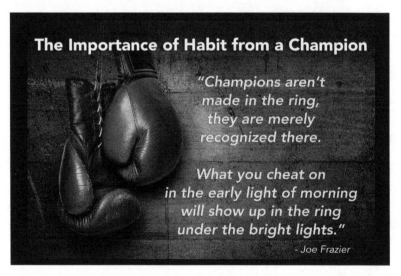

The Importance of Habit from a Champion

"Champions aren't made in the ring, they are merely recognized there.

What you cheat on in the early light of morning will show up in the ring under the bright lights."

- Joe Frazier

"What do you think that means, Frank?" asked The Wizard.

"If you are in the habit of doing the right things, like having a positive attitude, holding yourself accountable, progressively improving and actively listening to your customers while being in their operating reality, you are taking a huge step towards becoming the only choice," responded Frank. "It's kind of like back in my wrestling days. If I cheated on my morning runs or sometimes even skip a run, those bad habits would eventually show up when it was show time. And I would be on the short end of the stick!" Frank was clearly getting it now.

"Very good, Frank!" said The Wizard, impressed. "All great coaches profess a sincere desire to achieve what they refer to as muscle memory with their athletes. That means having the ability to naturally react to a situation correctly every single time. This is done through constant practice, drilling situations over and over again, and reinforcing the right habits to achieve the desired results. The thirteen things you wrote on that board are critical to your developing a salesperson's version of muscle memory — or good habits, if you will," explained The Wizard as he looked at his watch.

"It's 1:10 PM now, and we are moving into one of the most critical phases of today's session — process management and understanding customer relationships. We'll talk about this until about 2:45 PM or so and then take a break. Does that work?" asked The Wizard.

"That would be great!" said Frank enthusiastically. "I sure would like to be able to position myself to become the only choice!"

Chapter 4:
Understanding Process

The Wizard was a great believer that for any salesperson to become truly successful, he or she needed to have a basic understanding of process management and customer relationship management. Similar to football, how effectively can anyone play the game without a playbook? Put into a sales perspective, this means knowing where you are in the sales process as well as where the customer is in the buying/decision process and understanding where you are in terms of your relationship with the customer.

The Wizard's research over the past ten years indicated that nearly 98% of companies teach their salespeople the sales process as a way to drive business with their customers. Although there is some variation from company to company with respect to exactly what is contained in each step of the sales process, he believed that in almost all cases it is an internally focused process designed to drive sales, and not necessarily designed to create value for customers.

"Frank," The Wizard asked, "Can you explain to me the sales process that you have been taught at Standard?"

"Do you mind if I use the whiteboard?" asked Frank, as he grabbed a marker.

"Not at all," replied The Wizard. "Be my guest."

Frank started drawing boxes outlining each step of the sales process:

"Can you explain what each of the steps means?" asked The Wizard.

Frank thought to himself, "*What an odd request. The Wizard has spent thirty years in sales, and he needs me to explain each step of the sales process?*"

"Sure," he replied. "I'll spell each step out on the board as well." Frank wrote:

- <u>Prospecting:</u> Cold calling a specific territory or accounts in an effort to develop opportunities to sell products and services.

- <u>Qualifying:</u> Determining whether the contacts at the prospective company actually used and/or had the authority to purchase products and services on behalf of the company.

- <u>Customer Meetings:</u> Arranging face-to-face meetings with the intent to be able to gain a commitment to provide a proposal for goods and services.

- <u>Proposal:</u> A written document providing the customer with specific information about products and services you provide, including pricing, delivery, specifications, etc.

- <u>Close:</u> The "art" of gaining a customer commitment or securing an order.

"Thank you, Frank, well done. You clearly have a good handle on the sales process," said The Wizard.

The praise made Frank feel good about his ability to clearly articulate Standard's sales process step by step, and the meaning of each step. The good feeling, however, would be short-lived.

"Is this the process you used with your contact at The Wheeler Company?" asked The Wizard.

"Yes, it was, I guess," Frank said sheepishly, remembering that not-so-successful call. "I didn't really think about it."

"So…you got to the customer meeting stage and started pitching a Total Cost Reduction program — correct?" asked The Wizard.

"Uh, uh, yes," stammered Frank, realizing The Wizard was probably going to make a point that would more than offset that good feeling he had just moments earlier.

"And were you successful?" asked The Wizard, already knowing the answer to his own question, of course.

"Hmm, I think we have now established for the second time, in our brief time together, that it was not a successful sales call," replied Frank, becoming a bit irritated.

"What do you think went wrong with that process?"

asked The Wizard. He was pushing Frank to apply what he learned so far.

"Well, based on what I have learned this morning, I was not in the customer's operating reality," Frank said, "and I made no effort to understand if there was *GAP* between Wheeler's desired state with their current program and their actual state."

"So, you were not able to find the customer's pain, were you?" asked The Wizard.

"Obviously not!" responded Frank, annoyed with the line of questioning. "It is crystal clear that I was not in the customer's operating reality. I get it, already. So, instead of rehashing this over and over again, how do I force myself to stay in the customer's operating reality?" asked Frank. He was desperately trying to understand so he that he didn't make the same mistake again. And he was starting to feel a little beaten up over the Wheeler call.

"Fair question, Frank," replied The Wizard. "You see, this sales process is an internally focused process designed for the needs of the salesperson and the salesperson's company. Sales focused processes rarely take into consideration the customer's needs. They primarily focus on sales activities.

It reminds me of a story about a new salesperson and his manager that goes like this: The manager tells the new salesperson,

"Kid, sales is a numbers game! The more calls you make the more opportunities you have. The more opportunities

you have, the more orders you get. Understand, kid?"
The new salesperson nods his head. The sales manager
tells him, "Now, go out there and make some cold calls!"
At the end of the day the new salesperson comes back in
the office and tells the sales manager he made 99 calls
that day. The sales manager praises the young lad for a
great effort. The kid says, "I would have made 100, but
someone actually wanted to know what I had to say."

"Wow, that is sad," said Frank. He realized he had similar management experiences like that one.

"Yes, it is sad," agreed The Wizard. "And I can guarantee you somewhere today, some new hire is being coached by his manager just like that."

The Wizard then decided to turn his attention to the Customer Buying/Decision Process and asked Frank, "Do you understand the Buying/Decision Process and what it looks like through the customer's eyes?"

"I am not sure that I do," replied Frank. He also wanted to understand where The Wizard was going with this question.

The Wizard got up and walked towards the whiteboard, saying, "Let me show you what I mean." He then wrote on the whiteboard:

The Buying/Decision Process as it looks through your customer's Operating Reality:

| Identify Need | ⇒ | Investigate Options | ⇒ | Resolve Concerns | ⇒ | Purchase/ Decision | ⇒ | Implement |

The Wizard believed sales people needed to have a clear understanding of how customers made decisions, and specifically what The Buying/Decision Process looked like through the customer's operating reality. Although The Wizard referred to the process as The Buying/ Decision Process, he understood that it was really a decision process with which any decision could be made effectively. He called it The Buying/Decision Process so that he could emphasize to his students that they must look at the process through their customer's eyes.

Frank's eyes opened wide as he thought about this new concept.

"This, Frank, is the customer's buying or decision-making process," The Wizard began. "It starts with the *Identify Need phase, moves to Investigate Options, Resolve Concerns, Purchase/Decision and concludes with Implement.*"

"That makes perfect sense to me," said Frank, marveling at the simplicity and wondering why in three years of sales this was the first time he was seeing things from the customer's perspective.

"I like to teach things from a process perspective because it allows for faster learning. Let's break down each stage of the process so we can see the impact a consultative salesperson, working in the customer's operating reality, can make," said The Wizard, as he began to write descriptions for each phase in simple, easy-to-understand terms.

- <u>Identify Need</u>: The customer realizes there is GAP between desired state and actual state. This can be caused by dissatisfaction or by a salesperson helping their customer to understand their needs in a new or different way.

- <u>Investigate Options</u>: In this stage, the customer evaluates competing alternatives. This can be done formally via a Request for Proposal or informally through meetings with different competing companies.

- <u>Resolve Concerns</u>: In this stage, customers typically raise objections (real or tactical) to help justify their decision. While negotiation can and does take place in each of the stages, this is typically where final negotiations take place.

- <u>Purchase/Decision</u>: The customer makes a decision and awards the business.

- <u>Implement</u>: The customer begins implementation of the product, program or service, or in less complex sales, simply uses or consumes the product or service.

"Does this help you with a better understanding of each of the stages of the customer's Buying/Decision Process?" asked The Wizard.

"Yes, it sure does," replied Frank.

"Now understand, Frank," offered The Wizard, "we are all customers at one time or another since we purchase things practically every single day. For larger purchases, we may move through this process more slowly and perceive the beginning and end of each stage. For smaller purchases, we may move from Identification of Needs to Purchase without batting an eye."

"Understood."

"To be sure that you do understand, I would like to share with you a quick and simple story to help you to understand the stages of the process better," said The Wizard.

"A man is driving home from work and he notices a sign at the local Quick Mart that says Milk: $.99 per gallon, as he drives past. *"That's cheap,"* he thinks to himself.

"Milk is usually $3.25 per gallon." About twenty minutes later his cell phone rings as he is about a mile from home. It's his wife asking him to pick up milk on his way home. What stage of the Buying/Decision Process is the man in right at that moment?" asked The Wizard.

"Obviously, he is now in the *Identify Need* stage," replied Frank.

"Correct!" responded The Wizard. "Now the man remembers the milk that was priced at $.99 about twenty miles back. He sees there is a Kroger's store up ahead on the right as well as a Seven-Eleven store. What stage of the Buying/Decision Process is he in now?" asked The Wizard.

"*Investigate Options*," responded Frank confidently. This was almost too easy.

"Correct!" exclaimed The Wizard. "He mulls over the

options and decides not to drive back twenty miles to buy the cheaper milk, narrowing his choice to either the Kroger's or the Seven-Eleven. He thinks to himself, 'All I need is milk and I am almost home. Even though Kroger is about $.75 cheaper than Seven-Eleven, I know I am probably going to get stuck in a line behind someone pulling out their checkbook after the sale is already rung up. Meanwhile, I can be in and out in less than two minutes at the Seven-Eleven.'

"What stage is the man at now?" asked The Wizard.

"Clearly the *Resolve Concerns* stage," replied Frank. He was becoming bored with the simplicity of this exercise.

"Correct," said The Wizard, ignoring Frank's attitude. "In the *Resolve Concerns* phase, he is clearing any obstacles to purchase, deciding that **Value = Benefits – Cost**. In his mind, it is worth the $.75 price difference for the convenience of being able to get in and out of the store in less than two minutes. Notice he did not buy on price! He makes his decision to purchase the milk at Seven-Eleven, and then he drinks the milk with his family at dinner — which in effect are the *Purchase* and *Implement* phases of the Buying/Decision process. Does this make sense to you, Frank?"

"Yes, it is unbelievably simple," commented Frank. "I bet you can break down every buying decision and move it through this process. Clearly, if you can do it with milk, you can do it with a Total Cost Reduction Program. But how do you get the customer to the *Identify Need* phase? I mean, the milk purchase was a good example to understand the process a customer goes through, but suppose a customer is happy with his current situation and has no needs?"

"Fair question, Frank," said The Wizard. "Let's start by breaking down each step of the process like you did with your sales process and see if we can't help you answer that question."

The Wizard walked over to the whiteboard and began to write on the third of the three whiteboard panels, directly across from where Frank had written his interpretation of the sales process.

He started by drawing out the Buying/Decision process step by step, highlighting the first box.

Next, The Wizard wrote on the board:

- <u>Identify Needs</u>: The consultative seller can create more value early in the process by helping customers define needs in a new or different way.

- <u>Investigate Options</u>: The consultative seller can design a customized solution, helping the customer make better, more informed choices.

- <u>Resolve Concerns</u>: The consultative seller can act as a Trusted Advisor by counseling the customer, helping them to resolve concerns.

- <u>Purchase/Decision</u>: The consultative seller can make the purchase simple and hassle-free.

- <u>Implement</u>: The consultative seller can work to solve any implementation issues.

"So… let's start with the *Identify Need* stage and the consultative seller's impact on it," proposed The Wizard.

"The customer typically arrives at this point when there is GAP between desired state and actual state. In other words, there is an element of dissatisfaction on the customer's part," continued The Wizard. "The objective of the salesperson in this phase of the process is to create value for the customer by helping him or her to understand needs or problems in a different way."

"And how exactly is that accomplished, Jack," asked Frank; It sounded easy, but Frank was wondering how complex this discussion was going to get.

"Good question, Frank," responded The Wizard. "But before I answer that question, could I ask you a couple of questions?"

"Sure, fire away," replied Frank, wondering why The Wizard needed to ask him questions.

"You are married, right, Frank?" asked The Wizard, noticing the wedding band on Frank's left hand.

"Yes, I am," responded Frank. "It will be two years next month."

"How did you and your wife meet, if you don't mind me asking?" said The Wizard, obviously interested in the story.

"No, I don't mind at all," said Frank. Like most people, he liked talking about himself and was happy to share the story. "We met in college at the student union. I was a sophomore and Carmen was a freshman. It was the St. Patrick's Day gala. She was working the door with her friend, collecting the money, and a buddy of mine and I were working the door checking for college IDs. I liked her and my friend working the door with me liked her friend, as well. In an effort to get their attention, I decided to be creative and told the students in line that if they showed me their Prom pictures, they would get free admission. Next thing you know, everyone started showing us his or her Prom pictures to get in free. When the students pointed at us saying we authorized the free admission, Carmen and her friend laughed and said we couldn't do that."

Frank continued, knowing this was a good story. "So we had a good laugh and stopped asking to see Prom pictures in exchange for free admission. At the end of the night, I asked Carmen to show me her Prom picture. When she showed it to me, I asked if it was her old boyfriend in the picture. Carmen was quick to inform me that it was not only her old boyfriend but her current boyfriend as well."

"What did you say after that?" asked The Wizard. "I asked her if her boyfriend attended the university with her," replied Frank.

"Did he?" asked The Wizard. He was not letting on that he had heard the entire story from Al prior to their meeting.

"No, he was back home, about 90 miles away, and she said she went home every weekend to see him," replied Frank.

"So, I explained to her that the weekends offered some of the best times in college and that she was only getting about 65% of the college experience. She had no idea that she was missing so much until I pointed it out to her that night. And to make a long story short, she stayed at the university the following weekend and we bumped into each other at a concert. We had a great time — just as friends. I, of course, asked her out, and she said she couldn't because of the boyfriend. The following week, I met her again at the student union and asked her how she and her boyfriend were doing, and that's when she told me they broke up."

"Did you ask her out again on the spot?" asked The Wizard.

"Yes, I did," replied Frank. "We went out that Thursday night and the rest is history!"

"Wow, that's a great story. I particularly like the way you brought her to *Identify Needs* — helping her to understand her needs in a new or different way."

"What?" exclaimed Frank. Lost in his memories, he suddenly realized The Wizard had made reference to The Buying/Decision Process.

"You know, the way you clearly created *GAP* between the desired state and the actual state," said The Wizard. "You helped her to understand she wasn't enjoying the full college experience because she went home every weekend. You created a *GAP* in her mind. Here you were, this nice guy interested in her, and you weren't 90 miles away. You probably had more in common with her than her old boyfriend anyway because of the shared college experience, so once she understood that she was at the *Identify Need* phase, and she saw you as a viable option..."

Frank interrupted, "You are not comparing my marriage to the Buying/Decision Process are you, Jack?"

"In a way, yes. In a way, no. I did see it as an opportunity to prove a point. By staying top of mind with Carmen — that is, by keeping her aware of your presence and by asking questions to get to know Carmen and her situation better, you were able to help her clearly understand her needs in a new or different way. It just so happens that the value you were creating for her was you! See, I knew you had it in you!" exclaimed The Wizard.

"Okay, okay, I get your point, Jack," Frank jumped in. "But let's talk about when the customer is totally happy with the current situation. How do you create value for the customer then?"

"First, to bring a customer to the *Identify Need* phase, you must have a strong grasp of the four different types of questions in order to seek to understand," offered The Wizard. He asked Frank to remember Lesson #1, pointing to the card on the table:

LESSON #1

Seek to understand
before asking to be understood.[2]

2. Stephen R. Covey, *Seven Habits of Highly Successful People*, First Edition

"There are four types of questions you need to ask in order to bring a customer to an Identification of Needs," continued The Wizard, as he began to write on the whiteboard:

Situation: These questions are used to gather information to define a customer's current situation. The answers can consist of facts, data, etc.

Insight: These are questions that help you — and the customer — to see beyond the obvious and start to create GAP between the customer's actual state and desired state. You may see the GAP but the customer may not.

GAP: These are questions that help customers see that there is a clear GAP between their desired state and actual state and start them thinking about taking action.

Needs/Solution: These are questions that feed off the Value = Benefits – Cost formula and help the customer recognize the value of moving the discussion forward and understanding proposed solutions.

"As you can see, Frank," said the Wizard, pointing to the first letter of each word, "when you look at the first letter of each type of question, the acronym spells out the word *SIGN*. In today's competitive environment, we need to be searching for the *SIGN* questions on every sales call. Using the *SIGN* questions keeps good sales people focused on understanding not only what they know, but also what they don't know about a customer's current operation. Remember, Frank, it's not what you know that hurts you with respect to customers. It's what you don't know. The *SIGN* questions are designed to be an integral part of a structured, repeatable methodology to help you learn what you don't know."

Frank thought for a moment. "I have heard of *SIGN* questions. Al mentioned something in passing about the types of questions he was asking customers, just like the four types of questions you have put on the board. I just didn't put two and two together."

"Good," said The Wizard. He was pleased that Frank had come into the session with some knowledge of the *SIGN* questions. "We will use these questions to help answer your question about how we can create value for a customer who appears to be totally happy with the current supplier, okay, Frank?" asked The Wizard.

"Okay, let's have at it," replied Frank, excited about getting into the nitty-gritty.

"First," said The Wizard, "we need to go back to how we create *'GAP'* for our customers to drive home a visual understanding of what the *Identification of Need* phase looks like." The Wizard pointed to the drawing he had done earlier. He then modified the drawing to clearly illustrate how *SIGN* questions help to bring a customer to a *Identification of Needs* stage in the Buying/Decision Process.

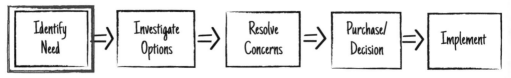

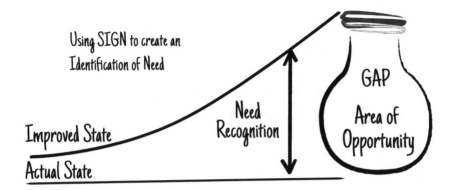

Using SIGN to create an Identification of Need

Improved State

Actual State

Need Recognition

GAP

Area of Opportunity

"As you can see, Frank," The Wizard began, "in this case there is no *GAP* between the customer's perception of desired state and actual state."

"I see," acknowledged Frank, curious to see how The Wizard was going to create *GAP* and bring the hypothetical customer to a *"Identification of Needs."*

"If the customer believes that there is no difference between the desired state and actual state, your only option is to add a new dimension to the current level of value they are receiving," continued The Wizard.

"New dimension?" asked Frank. "What do you mean by a new dimension?"

"A new dimension is the ability to create value above and beyond the customer's desired state. There are many excellent examples of this in the product development world. In the early to mid-eighties, customers did not know they needed a facsimile machine to transmit documents instantly. Most were happy with guaranteed overnight service," explained The Wizard. "When the prospect of receiving hard copy documents immediately became available, *GAP* was created between desired state and actual state. Fax machines were the solution to fill that *GAP*. A new dimension can be achieved through asking the right questions and by helping the customer understand their needs in a new or different way."

"Point well taken," acknowledged Frank, "but I am not a product development engineer."

"Well, it can be as simple as what you shared with me about how you and Carmen got together," The Wizard reminded him. "It appeared to me by the way you told the story that Carmen believed her actual state and her desired state were one and the same. By asking her questions about her current situation and raising the issue of the distance between her and her boyfriend, you were able to create *GAP* by adding a new dimension: the fact that she was only receiving about 65% of the total college experience."

"Good point," acknowledged Frank. "But that worked in a personal relationship. What I am trying to understand is how it would work in a business relationship."

"No problem, Frank," said The Wizard. "But keep in mind the principles are the same. Business relationships mirror personal relationships in a lot of ways. In fact, they can be one in the same."

Frank nodded in agreement.

"So, back to your meeting with The Wheeler Company," suggested The Wizard. "How much did you know about them prior to the sales call?"

"Not a whole lot," Frank admitted. "I mean, I knew they were a large financial services company, headquartered in New York. I knew the name of one of the key decision makers because he did a small amount of business with Standard several years ago. When I called to see if he was still there and found out that he was, I asked if I could stop by and introduce myself. I guess since he was familiar with Standard, he said okay."

"And you did no pre-call research on the company, the players, the financial condition?" asked The Wizard.

"Uh, no, I guess I didn't," Frank was very embarrassed about having to admit this. "I just reviewed what was in the file and what we had in our system in terms of history."

"Okay, Frank, before we go any further, you need to do some research on The Wheeler Company. Why don't you use my computer and see what you can find?" offered The Wizard. "Meanwhile, I will take a quick walk to the corner store to pick up a few things." The Wizard put on his coat and headed for the door. "Be back in twenty!" he said.

Frank made his way over to the computer and Googled The Wheeler Company. Wheeler was a publicly held company with annual sales of just over $1 billion, and they were one of the largest financial printers in the U.S. with eighteen manufacturing facilities nationwide. Wheeler's sales had been in decline the past three years to the tune of nearly 20%. Profits were declining at a more rapid rate — nearly 30%. The CEO had attributed a significant portion of the decline to the economy and alternative uses of technology; however, Frank knew that at least two of their competitors were growing in spite of the economy and technology. Frank was able to understand Wheeler's vision and mission, as well as the four priorities for the company for the fiscal year — with the main focus revolving around improved customer retention via improved quality and operational excellence.

He then began to search on his contact through a number of social sites whereby he could see his entire professional career, common connections and how he described his role.

As promised, The Wizard returned about twenty minutes later, and Frank got up and met him back over at the seating area armed with a lot of new information and insight into the wants and needs of Wheeler at the macro level.

"So what did you learn about Wheeler's current situation?" asked The Wizard.

"I probably need to start by saying that Wheeler is not a financial services company. They are a printer specializing in financial printing — secure documents, checks, annual reports, etc.," muttered Frank, embarrassed that he had had so little knowledge about the company. "How could I have been so stupid as to not research the company up front? I mean, with all the information available to me, I didn't even have enough smarts to use it."

"Frank," said The Wizard, "how much do you think that sales call cost your company?"

"I have no idea," responded Frank, without giving it much thought.

"Well, let me share something with you. One of the companies I recently worked with allowed me to measure the cost of one of their sales calls," shared The Wizard. "The company said that the sales professional earned $80,000 per year, and when they added benefits, bonuses, infrastructure costs, corporate overhead the fully loaded cost was approximately $160,000 per year. This sales professional received three weeks' vacation each year, and she made approximately seven face-to-face sales calls per week. The fully-loaded cost associated with each of these sales calls in the most basic way was..." The Wizard walked over to the whiteboard, erasing some of the information to create space and began to write the following as he talked it through.

$$7 \text{ sales calls} \times 49 \text{ weeks} = 343 \text{ sales calls,}$$
$$\text{divided into } \$160,000 = \$466$$

"Oh, no!" exclaimed Frank, now more embarrassed than before. "I know, my sales calls aren't costing the company that much but based on the way you are calculating the cost, it is probably close to $400!"

"Do you understand where I am going with this?" asked The Wizard.

"Absolutely," replied Frank. "You are going to show

theoretical money spent with no return on investment."

"Yes and no," responded The Wizard. "Yes, there was virtually no return on investment; and no, the money was not theoretically spent — IT WAS SPENT!"

"You see, Frank," The Wizard began, "we have access to a finite amount of time and a finite amount of capital. There is not an endless supply of each. A year measured in minutes is 525,600 minutes. A business year, based on working 40 hours per week for 50 weeks per year is 120,000 minutes. When you consider what you cost your company per year — and if you buy into the old adage that "time is money" — you can quickly calculate costs and provide a return on investment for everything you do. Sort of an activity-based costing, if you will. Are you following me, Frank?" asked The Wizard using his famous response check to test for understanding.

"Yes, I am," replied Frank. He grasped the concept but wanted to use a little response check of his own. "What you are saying is that by not doing a good job planning sales calls and doing customer research up front for the Wheeler call, I basically burned nearly $400 of my company's money and my valuable time with no return on that investment, right?"

"Dead on!" shouted The Wizard, pleased that Frank had grasped the concept so quickly. "Not to mention," he continued, "the intangible lost opportunity cost you had with the customer in terms of their perception of you and Standard. Unfortunately for both you and the Standard Company, the customer's perception of you at this point is probably not very good."

"True," admitted Frank. He hadn't thought about it from that angle. "It's amazing to me that I have achieved even mediocre sales status given all of the bad habits I am presently operating with. It sure didn't take you long to illustrate them to me today."

"Frank, Frank, Frank." said The Wizard, "You are not the first and only salesperson to make some of these basic mistakes, and trust me, you will not be the last. We have all been there," The Wizard said, reassuringly.

"Even you have made these mistakes in your past?" asked Frank. He was somewhat astonished, since he viewed The Wizard as a star, and anxiously awaited the answer to his question.

"Every single one of them!" proclaimed The Wizard without hesitation. "How do you think I got to where I am today?" He referred Frank to one of the wisdom statements on the wall, which simply said:

> Good judgement comes from experience...
> and experience comes from bad judgement.

"Yeah," responded Frank, though he didn't feel much better. He remembered Al shared that with him at dinner last week. "It makes a lot of sense... if and only if you truly do learn from your mistakes."

"True," agreed The Wizard. He could sense Frank's attitude slipping again. "Frank, let me help you to understand the way of the world a little better, and perhaps it will help you to better understand your sales journey. First, a question: did you ever wonder why the rearview mirror of a car is this big," asked The Wizard, holding his hands about eight inches apart, "and the windshield is this big?" holding his hands as far apart as they could go.

Frank just stared at The Wizard, pondering what he considered a somewhat bizarre question, not knowing exactly how to respond.

"You see, Frank," offered The Wizard, "you can draw a parallel between the whole concept of perseverance and progressive improvement with driving a car. We gain hindsight — or experience, if you will — by glancing in the rearview mirror, looking at all that went before. All that you see in that rearview mirror is now history, and this means that we are learning from both our successes and our failures. At the same time, we look ahead through the windshield, at the possibilities that lie before us. We gain foresight and vision by imagining a better future ahead — by learning from our mistakes. This approach calls for us to live in the present, worrying about neither yesterday nor tomorrow, but rather, striving for continued and balanced improvement every single day, boldly and passionately facing the challenges that tomorrow offers."

Frank marveled at The Wizard's wisdom. "Clearly," he

thought, "this is a man who understands life, work and in particular, what I am going through as a mediocre salesperson aiming to be at the level of a President's Roundtable Member."

"Do you understand what I am saying?" asked The Wizard.

"Yes sir, I do," acknowledged Frank. "It is crystal clear."

The Wizard now felt that Frank was starting to buy in to the program. His defense mechanisms were disabled, and his mind was completely open and willing to learn. Frank, for his part, knew he was staring at a crossroads in his sales career, and he was, unequivocally, looking right smack at a defining moment.

"I am really looking forward to learning more." Frank felt as though he was coming to grips with his shortcomings — shortcomings he didn't even realize he had when he got in that taxi a few short hours ago.

"It's 2:30 PM now, Frank. Why don't we take a fifteen minute break and then pick up with the *SIGN* questions and The Buying/Decision Process?" suggested The Wizard.

"Do you mind if I take a walk around the block?" asked Frank. He felt a need to clear his head. They had covered a lot of ground.

"No, go right ahead. The cold, fresh air will do you good!" exclaimed The Wizard. "While you do that, I will check my messages and return some phone calls. Take your time."

Frank put on his coat and stepped outside, braving the cold New York weather. As he began his walk around the block, listening to the ever-present Manhattan background of horns beeping and smelling the fumes of what seemed like a million cars, Frank, remembered what The Wizard said as he walked out the door. He thought to himself, *"Cold air, maybe. Fresh air — no way!"*

While making the final turn around the block, Frank made a commitment to himself that he would be a model student when he returned and work hard to keep his attitude in line. As he visualized all the mistakes he had made in his nearly three-year sales career, he could clearly attribute those mistakes to his attitude, a lack of preparation, not being in the customer's operating reality, not asking the right types of questions, not actively listening, not being accountable — basically, everything The Wizard said was important. *"I have made all these mistakes,"* Frank thought to himself, *"and I am a mediocre salesperson. My God, what does a bad salesperson look like? What a horrifying thought!"*

When Frank returned to the apartment, The Wizard was finishing up yet another call with a Standard salesperson, discussing account strategy. As he hung up the phone, Frank asked, "Another strategy session?"

"Yes, you could say that," responded The Wizard, as he quickly changed the subject back to Frank. "Feeling better?" he asked.

"Yes, I am, and I apologize if I gave you the impression I was feeling sorry for myself," responded Frank. "The truth is, though, I kind of was feeling sorry for myself. But on my brief walk, I thought a lot about what we have covered today, and I am ready to move on, focusing on what's ahead through that windshield."

"Don't worry about it. Let's get started again," said The Wizard. "You wanted to learn how to bring a satisfied customer to an *Identification of Needs* using effective questions, right?"

"That is correct," replied Frank. "You had just asked me what more I learned about Wheeler before we went off on a very valuable tangent."

"Okay, tell me what else you know about them" directed The Wizard, pleased with Frank's renewed energy and sincerity.

Frank shared with The Wizard what he had written down from his computer search: "Wheeler is a publicly held company with annual sales of just over $1 billion, and is one of the largest financial printers in the U.S. with eighteen manufacturing facilities nationwide. Wheeler's sales have been in decline for the past three years to the tune of nearly 20%. Profits are declining at a more rapid rate — nearly 30%. The CEO attributed a significant portion of the decline to the economy and alternative uses of technology; however, I know that at least two of their competitors are growing in spite of the economy and technology. I also was able to understand Wheeler's vision and mission as well as the four priorities for the company this fiscal year. Their main focus revolves around improved customer retention via improved quality and operational excellence."

"That's a good start!" replied The Wizard enthusiastically. "Any information about the key decision makers?"

"Yes. My contact reports directly to the Vice President of Operations," Frank said, wishing he had had this information prior to his meeting with Wheeler. He has been there for four years and we have two common connections. I will be reaching out to one of those common connections tomorrow to see if I can get some better insight on my contact."

"Good, Frank. Now, what are your primary and secondary objectives for a Wheeler sales call?"

"I am not totally sure yet," said Frank. His answer reflected that he did not have complete clarity and was looking for some help with the question.

"Okay, Frank," began The Wizard, as he handed Frank a single sheet of paper. "This is a call planning worksheet. It will help you structure your sales call in a logical manner and begin to gather the information and insight you need to create value for your customer."

"You mean to bring them to an *Identification of Needs*?" asked Frank, as he looked over the document.

"Exactly," replied The Wizard, pleased that Frank was able to tie the concept of value creation to bringing a customer to an *Identification of Needs*.

CALL PLANNING WORKSHEET

Organization		Contact	
Stage of Decision Process		Date	
CPW Owner		Participants	

Background/Interesting facts

Notes/Background Info	

Goal

Primary Goal	
Secondary Goal	

Fact Finding

Questions that will help achieve the primary/secondary goals.

Situation questions	
Insight questions	
Gap questions	
Needs/solution questions	
Summarize needs	

Anticipated Objections

Likely objections to overcome using LAER—	

"Frank," began the Wizard, "it has been my experience that sales people are generally among the worst planners I have ever seen. They often begin their call planning when they hit the off-ramp on their way to visit a prospective customer."

"Agreed," acknowledged Frank. "I am probably – no, wait, I *am* living proof of that."

The two men chuckled in agreement.

"The customer is willing to invest in the salesperson by giving him or her one of his most precious commodities – time." The Wizard continued, "The least we, as sales professionals can do in return is to respect that customer's time by taking the time to plan an effective sales call with a goal of bringing the customer to an *Identification of Needs*."

"I see," said Frank. "It makes perfect sense to me now. In fact, when I think about it, I used to use something like this when I first started selling. I mean, it didn't have the *SIGN* questions on it, but it did have primary and secondary objectives, as well as anticipated objections and my responses to them."

"Why did you stop using it?" asked The Wizard, curious to hear Frank's answer.

"I thought it was for novice sales people," replied Frank. "You know, a tool to get them started until they learn the business. I figured I knew enough that I didn't need it anymore."

"You see, Frank," offered The Wizard, "I view using the Call Planning Worksheet as good a habit, not a beginner's task. It should be what a successful salesperson is in the habit of using every day. After nearly 30 years in sales, I couldn't do without one."

"You still use the Call Planning Worksheet?" asked Frank. He was astonished that a seasoned veteran and successful salesperson like The Wizard would still use what he saw as such a basic tool.

"Yes, and to be honest with you, I believe that it is one of the main reasons I have been so successful," explained The Wizard. "It enables me to plan the sales call while being in the customer's *operating reality*. And therefore, my questions are targeted at creating value for the customer or, as we have learned today, bringing them to an *Identification of Needs*."

"How about when you went on joint sales calls, like with your boss?" asked Frank. "Weren't you concerned that it made you look like you didn't have your act together?"

"Quite the contrary, Frank. Let me tell you a quick story about using the Call Planning Worksheet. Several years back, I was preparing to call on one of my largest customers. The CEO at the time, Jim Beasley, was going to be on the sales call doing some executive bridging with the customer. I e-mailed Jim a Call Planning Worksheet reflecting the primary and secondary objectives of the call. I then listed the *SIGN* questions I wanted him to ask and the ones I would ask. I listed the anticipated objections and the appropriate responses. In addition, I provided background information on all of the players that would be at the meeting."

"What did he do?" asked Frank, wondering if The Wizard had offended the CEO by telling him what to do.

"He stopped by my office and asked me why I sent him the Call Planning Worksheet. He asked if I clearly understood that he was the CEO, and that he had his own style for customer sales calls."

"And what did you say?" asked Frank, thinking to himself, "Uh-oh, here it comes!"

"I listened to what he had to say, and I told him that I appreciated his concern," began The Wizard. "I then asked him how many sales calls he had been on in the last month."

"No way! That was bold. What did he say?" asked Frank

"He said one," explained The Wizard. "I then explained to him that I had been on no less than twenty times that every single month of my career. I explained to him that I had tremendous respect for his position and the demands on his time. I also made him aware, tactfully of course, that a CEO's job is the ultimate general management position and that as a CEO, he is required to be knowledgeable in a lot of different areas. I explained to him that he hired me to be an expert at my level, and that was exactly why I sent the Call Planning Worksheet, a critical tool of my trade. I shared with him that based on my information and insight into the key players, the highest return on investment we could possibly achieve on this sales call – with his $600,000 a year base salary calculated into the total cost to make the sales call – would be achieved by working together off of the Call Planning Worksheet."

"Oh my gosh!" gasped Frank. "You didn't? You actually said all of that to the CEO? What happened?"

"I am sure he considered my track record and appreciated my challenging him. We did the call together, and he followed the Call Planning Worksheet to a tee," explained the Wizard. "He used his charismatic personality to win people over while conducting the entire meeting in the customer's operating reality. And we walked away with $800,000 in new business."

"You did?" Frank was still astonished at the confidence The Wizard had displayed in his conversation with the CEO. "What a great story!"

"It's not over yet," cautioned The Wizard. "After the call, as we rode down the elevator and reconvened in the lobby, the CEO was like a little kid, so very pleased with the way the meeting had gone, and in particular, the $800,000 commitment for additional business. His first question to me was, "Did I hit all the questions?" I told him I thought he had, and that he had done a great job on the sales call. He responded that it was the best sales call he could ever remember being on, and that he was now a firm believer in the value of the Call Planning Worksheet."

"Wow." Frank was impressed with both The Wizard's gutsy approach and the CEO's ultimate response to it. "If the CEO can endorse the Call Planning Worksheet, then so can I!"

"That's great, Frank," replied The Wizard. "Now, let's get back to business. What are your primary and secondary objectives for the Wheeler sales call?"

"I guess my primary objective is to help the customer understand his needs in a new or different way; that is, to bring him to an *Identification of Needs*. Having him agree to a discovery would be my primary objective," offered Frank.

"And while putting yourself in the customer's operating reality, what would be the secondary objective?" asked The Wizard.

"In the spirit of due diligence and understanding that the next stage of the Buying/Decision Process is the *Investigate Options* stage, I would think my secondary objective would be to advance the relationship. I would want to gain a deeper understanding of the customer's business and provide some viable options for them to improve their business performance," replied Frank. He was gaining confidence as he began to visualize the process in his mind. "Something that ensures the process keeps moving forward."

"That's good, Frank," acknowledged The Wizard. "You didn't immediately go for the quick hit. You are truly looking at things through the customer's *operating reality*. Now, what type of questions are you going to ask and what information are you looking for?"

"I am not totally sure yet," said Frank, admitting he did not yet have a complete understanding of the SIGN questions.

The Wizard decided it was time to pick up the pace. He only had about two hours left and needed to cover the SIGN questions, objection handling and the relationship pyramid. He could see that Frank was starting to put things together and seemed energized and ready to learn. The Wizard knew now was the time to hammer home the fundamentals.

He began by listing four types of value creation questions on the whiteboard:

- Situation questions
- Insight questions
- GAP questions
- Needs/Solution questions

"Okay, Frank," said The Wizard with marker in hand, "let's begin with *Situation* questions. *Situation* questions are designed to gain information, facts and data about the customer's existing situation. Why don't you give me a couple of examples of *Situation* questions you might ask?"

"Considering that my contact told me in our last meeting that he was on contract with another supplier and given the fact that I know more about the company's overall vision, mission and financial performance, I would probably ask the following," offered Frank reading off his sheet.

1. I understand you are currently on contract with your current supplier. When does the contract terminate?

2. What exactly is covered under the agreement?

"I would also like to ask if the contract has an early termination clause for convenience or performance," Frank added. "However, I would feel uncomfortable doing so until I can begin to establish some dissatisfaction or *GAP* between the customer's desired state and actual state."

"That's good, Frank," said The Wizard. "You are demonstrating a clear understanding of both relationship building and process. Keep in mind that you shouldn't ask too many *Situation* questions. *Situation* questions benefit you, not the customer. Too many *Situation* questions can irritate the customer; and understand, once you are able to establish *GAP*, you can always go back and ask another *Situation* question to help clarify the customer's options."

"Now, let's move to *Insight* questions," The Wizard continued. "*Insight* questions are designed to help you take current information available and see beyond the obvious. *Insight* questions lead with a statement about the customer's current situation and are followed with a question designed to learn about dissatisfaction, difficulties or problems the customer is experiencing. *Insight* questions are the first step in creating *GAP* or bringing the customer to an *Identification of Needs*. Why don't you share with me the *Insight* questions you would ask given what you know about the company and its existing situation?"

Frank responded with the following questions:

- I understand a key initiative within Wheeler is improved operational excellence resulting in higher quality and better customer retention. How are you doing relative to achieving your quality objectives through your current program?

- Your annual report indicates sales and profits have declined over the past three years. Where do you feel your current program is providing you with the quality you need to effectively increase revenue opportunities?

- Given the increased emphasis on operational excellence at The Wheeler Company, how satisfied are you with the value of your current program when you consider all the costs, including quality and customer attrition?

"Very good!" The Wizard congratulated Frank. "Why do you think it makes sense to front-load the questions with a statement about the current situation?"

"I didn't feel I had earned the right to ask such a direct question without reassuring the customer that I had researched the company and had a good handle on their key priorities," replied Frank.

"Excellent answer. It certainly shows an investment on your part and softens the direct nature of the second half of the question. My only caution is to make sure you have your facts straight and that you are able to reference where the information came from."

"Good advice," said Frank.

"One key point I failed to mention," offered The Wizard. "Please make every effort to make your *Insight* questions open ended vs. closed questions—yes/no. This gets your prospect talking. Remember, when they are talking, you are learning!"

"Makes perfect sense," Frank replied.

"Okay Frank," The Wizard went on. "Why don't we move on to the *GAP* questions? *GAP* questions are designed to do one of two things. First, it can help customers who already know they are experiencing problems or are in a situation where there is a clearly established gap between actual state and desired state. *GAP* questions help customers understand what negative impact, consequence or effect the problem is having on their business, causing them to want a solution to fill the *GAP*."

"Understood," replied Frank. "And the second thing?"

"For customers that appear to be totally satisfied," continued The Wizard. "*GAP* questions are designed to help them understand their needs in a new or different way. This is done by adding a new dimension or helping the 'satisfied' customer to the *Identification of Needs* stage of the Buying/Decision Process."

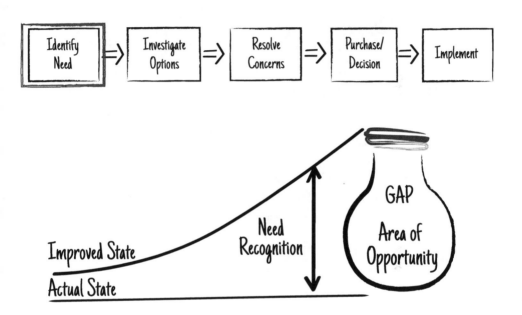

"Any examples you can share with me that would illustrate how this is done?" asked Frank.

"Absolutely," replied The Wizard. "I was just about to ask you to provide some examples. Let's start with a *GAP* question building off the *Insight* questions you asked earlier. Why don't you provide some examples of how you help the customer acknowledge there is *GAP* between actual state and desired state and why they need to do something about it?"

"Give me a couple of minutes to formulate them and write them on the whiteboard, okay?"

"No problem, Frank," replied The Wizard as he began to erase information from the whiteboard. "Take your time."

Frank was soon ready to share his *GAP* questions with The Wizard. Even The Wizard was impressed with how quickly Frank was learning to look for the signs and allowing the *SIGN* questions to guide him.

"Okay, I'm ready," declared Frank, as he wrote the following questions on the whiteboard:

- Given the fact that your current program is not meeting your quality goals, what impact has that had on customer retention?

- Considering that your current program is not meeting your quality objectives, how is that impacting your revenue goals?

"Very good, Frank. You seem to have a great handle on the first part of the *GAP* questions. Why didn't you address the third *Insight* question you listed earlier?" asked The Wizard.

"I was assuming the customer was satisfied, and I was going to use that as the basis for my new dimension *GAP* question," replied Frank, expressing a new level of confidence.

"Oh, you were, were you?" asked The Wizard,

acknowledging Frank's newfound confidence. "Well, I think you know where I am going to go next, so why don't we just get right to it? Why don't you give me a couple of examples of the second way to use *GAP* questions with a seemingly totally satisfied customer?"

Frank turned back to the whiteboard and began to script more questions on the board, all beginning with an appreciation of the customer's current situation.

- Well, I am happy to hear that both your operational excellence initiative and your current program are meeting their objectives in terms of slowing customer attrition. Given Wheeler's other primary initiative to get back to top line growth, suppose I could add a new dimension to the current level of service you are receiving that would offer increased revenue opportunities; would you be interested in taking the time to learn more?

- Well, I am happy to hear that your current program is meeting the operational excellence objectives resulting in less customer attrition. Suppose we could add a new dimension to the current level of service that you are receiving through Six Sigma quality standards and deliver increased revenue opportunities; would you be interested in learning more?

The Wizard just sat and looked at Frank. He could see Frank's transformation taking place right before his eyes. The Wizard marveled at how quickly Frank had moved from the tactical product selling approach he espoused only hours before to helping customers with improved solutions designed to help them improve their business performance.

"That's very good in theory, Frank," said The Wizard. "But do you think you can actually help them achieve the desired results?"

"I believe I can, if I have an opportunity to do a full-blown *Discovery*." Referring to the process by which Standard maps the customer's total program and looks for gaps between desired state and actual state.

"Let's face it, Jack, if I don't invest the time in the relationship, I'll never know if I can help. I have confidence that between my new-found effective questioning skills and working in the customer's *operating reality*, I have a better shot than most people at creating value for this customer."

"Well Frank, I am pleased that you see yourself creating value for this customer," replied The Wizard. "However, assuming you get him to consider the fact that there may be an opportunity to improve his current situation, how do you propose to gain commitment to move the conversation to the next level?"

"*Needs/Solution* questions," replied Frank confidently. "Once I get him to consider the possibility that things can be better, creating an open mind, I will use the *Discovery* process to bring him to an *Identification of Need*."

"Okay," asked The Wizard curiously. "How do you propose to do that?"

"Well, I assumed you were going to teach me!"
said Frank, laughing. "Hey, I have bought into your
philosophies hook, line and sinker, and I am feeling like a
new man! I am just waiting for some guidance from you
on the *Needs/Solutions* questions to take me over
the top!"

The Wizard was pleased with Frank's confidence.
He knew if he could provide Frank with a consistent
framework and process, Frank would flourish just as
Al did some three years earlier.

"Then let us move on to the *Needs/Solution* questions,"
said The Wizard. "A *Needs/Solution* question is only used
in the following situations." The Wizard walked over to
the whiteboard and began to write:

1. When the customer shares with you that, there are significant problems and issues in the current environment.

2. When GAP is clearly created between actual state and desired state through effective Insight questions and/or GAP questions.

3. When the customer shows interest in the 'new dimension' statement indicating a desire to improve the current situation even though it appears to be meeting his/her current needs.

"Keep in mind," explained The Wizard, "The *SIGN*
questions do not necessarily have to be asked in order.
Your sequence may look like this: S, S, I, S, I, I, S, G,
then move to a *Needs/Solution* question. The key to

everything is to ask the questions while in the customer's *operating reality*.

Frank was impressed with how consistent The Wizard was with his approach to sales, creating value and customer relationships. Very rarely did ten to fifteen minutes go by in any conversation about customers without The Wizard mentioning the term "*operating reality*."

Frank could only speculate how good a salesperson The Wizard actually was. He was a legend at The Standard Company, and after spending nearly a day with him, Frank could certainly appreciate his 'Wizard' status. He thought it would be terrific to actually go on a sales call with him. *"This guy brings unbelievable clarity and process to everything,"* Frank thought to himself. *"It's amazing I functioned at all without his guidance."* Frank could not help but daydream for a minute about what the future could be like. *"Could I end up achieving President's Roundtable status?"* he asked himself. *"Could I be as good as Al?*

While Frank was envisioning the possibilities that lay ahead, he found himself interrupted by one of The Wizard's patented response checks.

"Frank, do you understand what I mean about the sequencing of the questions?" asked The Wizard.

"Oh, uh, yes, Jack, I am crystal clear about it," responded Frank, recovering quickly from his little daydream. "I need to be actively listening and asking the questions in the appropriate sequence, not just in a predetermined order."

"Exactly. You want to be actively listening with your ears as well as listening with your eyes. By listening with your eyes, I mean picking up on any negative or positive body language that may enable you to adjust your sequence," explained The Wizard.

"Listening with my eyes?" Frank asked inquisitively. "I was always taught to listen with my ears and see with my eyes. Is that, not right?"

"Yes, Frank, that is correct in the basic sense," responded The Wizard. "But just like there is a difference – as we proved earlier – between listening and active listening, there is a difference between seeing and being able to process what you are seeing. I call that listening with your eyes."

"Understood," acknowledged Frank. "I need to make sure I am able to read the customer's body language and make the necessary adjustments to my approach."

"Exactly," acknowledged The Wizard. "So now let's move to how to use the *Needs/Solution* questions and effectively create the *Identification of Needs* in the mind of the customer. *Needs/Solution* questions are designed to advance the Buying/Decision Process and create the *Identification of Needs* in the mind of the customer. In your case with the Wheeler Company, you may have exposed *GAP* through either *Insight* questions or *GAP* questions. Now the job of the *Needs/Solution* questions is to clearly help the customer to understand that there is opportunity for improvement that it is significant enough to bring them to a *Identification of Needs*. The customer going through that simple equation:

Value = Benefits – Cost

"Therefore," continued The Wizard, "*Needs/Solution* questions are not solutions at all. *Needs/Solution* questions are questions designed to bring the customer to an *Identification of Needs* so that he or she will consider investing in the relationship in hopes of achieving a better solution."

"Invest in the relationship?" asked Frank. "What exactly do you mean by invest in the relationship? I thought they were investing in the relationship by meeting with me?"

"That is a form of investment on their part," explained The Wizard. "But now that you did not proceed to prescribe a solution before truly understanding what the problem was, and having legitimized yourself by seeking to understand, the next step is to ask the customer to invest more in you by asking more of them in terms of time, information and access to other people."

"I get it," said Frank. "This is where you don't go for the quick hit. Once you have the buyer interested and understanding that you are willing to invest more of your time and effort in them, you try to get them to invest in you as well."

"Right, Frank," replied The Wizard. "Now, given what you know about the Wheeler situation, why don't you take five minutes and put together a list of *Needs/Solution* questions you can ask, and write them on the whiteboard like you did with the other questions. To make sure we have clarity around the different types of *Needs/Solution* questions, ask the questions to address the different types of situations you may be in," said The Wizard, as he pointed to what he had written earlier.

1. When the customer shares with you that, there are significant problems and issues in the current environment.

2. When GAP is clearly created between actual state and desired state through effective Insight questions and/or GAP questions.

3. When the customer shows interest in the 'new dimension' statement indicating a desire to improve the current situation even though it appears to be meeting his/her current needs.

"No problem," replied Frank. "It will just take me a couple of minutes."

Frank seemed to be absorbing The Wizard's tutoring very well. His confidence was increasing with each passing hour. Frank was now totally engaged in the process and this new consultative approach to customers. As he wrote out his questions, he maintained one of the most critical aspects of the questioning process: he formulated his questions in the customer's operating reality.

Only a couple of minutes had passed when Frank said, "I am ready!"

"Okay. Let's see what you have."

Frank pointed to the first question:

    1. What would it mean to your company to improve customer retention by 5% and have it aligned with your operational excellence initiative? (Customer clearly has problems and has shared those problems with me.)

    2. If Wheeler could begin to achieve revenue growth of a modest 2%, what would that mean to the bottom-line?

"I only wrote two questions," offered Frank, "because I felt either one would work in all of the scenarios you described earlier. The goal is to get the customer to consider the possibilities of improving his current situation, and I felt either question would stimulate that type of thinking."

"This is excellent, Frank," acknowledged The Wizard. "You have the customer thinking that there is a real opportunity to improve the current situation. Assuming you perceived good body language and interest from the customer, where would you take the conversation next?" asked The Wizard.

"Now I would have to do more diagnosis via a *Discovery*, where I come back with specific questions and information needs to better assess the issues around his current situation," explained Frank. "I would need to have access to other people as well."

"Very good, Frank. I believe you have a good handle on the *SIGN* questions to create *GAP* in an effort to help the customer understand needs in a new or different way. Assuming you have brought the customer to *Identification of Needs*, let's move to basic objection handling and then we will get back to moving the customer through the Buying/Decision Process."

Chapter 5: Handling Customer Objections

The time was now 3:45 PM, and The Wizard knew he needed to speed things up. He began to speak to Frank about customer objections. He quickly got right to the point and opened with a question. "Do you like hearing objections from customers, Frank?" asked The Wizard.

"No," responded Frank, "Of course not. I can't imagine why anyone would like objections. They get in the way of your ability to move the process forward."

"Do they, Frank?" asked The Wizard. "Or do they actually enable you to move the process forward? There is a right way and a wrong way to look at customer objections. Sometimes customers use objections as tactics to try to influence your thinking. But most of the time, the customer simply has an issue or a problem understanding what you are presenting to him."

The first lesson was a simple one. The Wizard handed Frank a card:

An Objection
is merely a request
for more information.

Frank read the card The Wizard had handed him and thought to himself, *"That's certainly one way to look at it!"*

"Frank," continued The Wizard, "in most cases when customers put an objection out there, they are merely asking for more information to help them understand. It may not sound that way when you hear the objection, but most - and I mean 75% - of customer objections fall into this category. In addition, an objection can act as a window into the customer's *operating reality*; understanding and handling that objection effectively can give you a clear opportunity to set yourself apart from the competition."

"That makes sense," acknowledged Frank. "But how can you distinguish a real objection – that is, one that is requesting more information – from one that is a tactic to just shut you down?"

"Like with everything else we have discussed today," explained The Wizard, "and as you have probably guessed, there is a process for handling customer objections the right way."

"How did I know there would be another process?" smiled Frank. He was looking forward to starting the next lesson.

"The process is called *LAER*," continued The Wizard. "It stands for *Listen, Acknowledge, Explore,* then *Respond.*"

"LAER..." Frank said to himself. *"Sounds simple enough."*

"So, let's start with *Listen*. We talked earlier about listening versus active listening. By truly listening to the customer and reading body language, we are able to show empathy and illustrate to the customer that what he or she is saying is important. Does this make sense so far?"

"Absolutely!" Frank replied quickly. "It is consistent with everything else you have taught me today – as would be expected!"

"The next step is to *Acknowledge*," The Wizard went on. "By acknowledging, we are showing the customer we understand and that we can appreciate the customer's viewpoint. To *Acknowledge* may be something as simple as a head nod, changing the way you look at the customer to show more genuine interest, or leaning forward in your chair. You can also acknowledge the preferred way by saying something like 'I can appreciate your concern.'"

"What would you say is the most common form of acknowledgement?" asked Frank, leaning forward.

"I like to repeat back their objection so that they know that I understand their concern," shared The Wizard. "But I know others who leverage the use of using body language. You know, nodding their head or moving forward in their chair. I guess it depends on your style."

"Now let's move to the *Explore* stage of objection handling. Since most objections are very broad and wide, it is usually necessary to ask clarifying questions to make sure that we have a complete understanding of what the customer's true concern is. If you recall my story about our former CEO and the Call Planning Worksheet, I asked an *Exploratory* question about how many sales calls he had made in the last month before I responded to his objection about the Call Planning Worksheet. That was a good example of using *LAER* and demonstrating that an objection is usually a request for more information. But enough about that story. The most common objection we hear in sales is the price objection, right?"

"Certainly, one I am familiar with," replied Frank, "and one I don't handle very well, I might add."

"If you approach the price objection by understanding that it is merely a request for more information or a justification of sort, you will do a much better job of handling that objection," explained The Wizard. "What we will need to do is to ask an *Exploratory* question to make sure that price is truly the objection we are facing. Once the customer puts out the 'your price to too high' objection, we must listen, acknowledge, and ask at least one exploratory question before responding. It is not mandatory that *LAER* be done in exact sequence; however, most of the time it is done that way. Much like the *SIGN* questions, you may actually sequence the questions like this: *L, A, E, A, E, E, R.*"

"Obviously, if I am actively listening and I am in the customer's *operating reality*, then I would just follow the flow of the conversation," offered Frank, demonstrating his understanding of the *LAER* process.

"Exactly," acknowledged The Wizard. "The goal is to

have true understanding of the perceived objection before actually responding to it. So, moving back to the 'your price is too high' objection, why don't you and I role practice that objection?"

"Role-practice? I thought the term was role-playing?" asked Frank.

"We ain't playing!" quipped The Wizard. "I call it role-practice, because I want people to approach business and sales with the mindset of a competitive athlete. Practice is what athletes do to be successful. Role-practice is what sales people need to do to perfect their skills."

"I get it and it is music to my ears," agreed Frank, getting right into the role-practice by playing the buyer from Wheeler.

"I like what you have to offer, Jack. Unfortunately, it appears that your pricing is too high."

The Wizard leaned forward in his chair and said, "Well, I can certainly appreciate your desire to achieve the lowest price. But are we talking price or fully-loaded cost?"

"What do you mean by full-loaded cost?" asked Frank playing the role of the buyer.

"This is where even the best sales people give the buyer the answers to the test," offered The Wizard, stepping out of the role-practice. "They help the buyer by asking if it includes freight, maintenance, etc. Of, course the buyer says 'yes'!"

"As you are probably aware, there are many factors

beyond price. In your fully-loaded cost comparison, what other cost factors are in your cost analysis?" *Explored* The Wizard, back in role-practice mode.

"Fully loaded cost?" asked Frank. One part of him was still in the role-practice and one part was interested in understanding the term "fully loaded costs." "How would I measure fully loaded costs?"

"It can be done by calculating the total cost of ownership of the product. While our price per unit is a little bit higher, the total cost of ownership is significantly lower over the length of the contract, which will actually save you money," answered The Wizard in *Respond* mode.

"You see, Frank," explained the Wizard shifting out of the role-practice, "The customer's objection in this case was a request for more information. He only knew price and that was his only frame of reference. By asking a simple *Exploratory* question, I was able to understand that and provide the appropriate response to help the customer feel better about the higher price. Remember, the customer goes through a process that uses the formula, *Value = Benefits minus Cost.*"

"*L-A-E-R*," Frank spelled aloud admiring its simplicity. Another process I can learn to force good habits when dealing with customers.

"Jack, is there ever a time you do not ask an *Exploratory* question prior to *Responding*?

"I imagine it would be very rare. Just think about any objection a customer could possibly put forward. What would be wrong with asking a question to test for understanding? Asking an *Exploratory* question does two things. It forces you to narrow the objection so that you can understand it and handle it more effectively. And secondly, it keeps the customer talking which might provide more insight into the driving force behind the objection."

"I get it, Jack," acknowledged Frank. "*LAER* is a process that forces me to truly understand the customer's real objection before responding to it. And going back to the *SIGN* questions, I can use any one of those types of questions as my *Exploratory* question, right?"

"Right," agreed The Wizard. "Remember, an objection is merely a request for more information. By actively listening to your customers and their concerns, and acknowledging their concerns as legitimate, you are building trust and rapport. By asking an *Exploratory* question before responding to an objection, you are clearly seeking to understand before asking to be understood."

Moving through The Customer's Buying/Decision Process

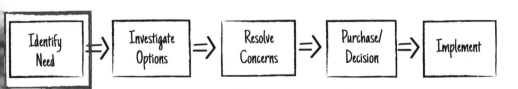

"Frank," began The Wizard, "we have spent a considerable amount of time on the first stage of the

Buying/Decision Process, because without creating *Identification of Needs*, the process stalls and goes nowhere."

"Just like my Wheeler sales call yesterday," Frank pointed out.

"Yes," agreed The Wizard. "Now once you have created *GAP* between the actual state and the desired state, there is an opportunity for a consultative salesperson such as yourself to act as a 'trusted advisor' and help your customer evaluate options and make better, more informed decisions."

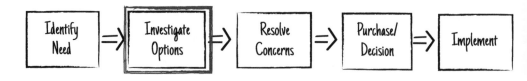

"If I have it correctly, as a trusted advisor to the customer, I must bring two critical components to the *Investigate Options* stage. First, I must have subject matter expertise and second, see the opportunities as they exist through the customer's eyes, not with my own commission in mind," offered Frank, demonstrating his ability to string all of his key learnings together in a logical way.

"Correct, Frank" said The Wizard, pleased that Frank had remembered the trusted advisor conversation from earlier in the day. They had covered a lot of ground in a fairly short time. "My studies indicate that if you are able to bring customers to *Identification of Needs* and move them through the process in your role as a trusted advisor, you will be awarded the business over 90% of the time."

"Is that a fact?" Frank was amazed at the high win percentage.

"Yes, it is," replied The Wizard. "I have tracked this statistic through the performance of each of my sales people over the past ten years and it is a fact that if you help the customer to a *Identification of Needs* stage, you will win 90% of the time. If you enter the process at the *Investigate Options* stage, it usually means someone else has brought them to *Identification of Needs* and the empirical data says you will only win 10% of the time."

"Can you give me an example of what it looks like when you get involved at the *Investigate Options* stage?" Frank was hoping to gain a clear understanding of this major revelation.

"Sure," said The Wizard. "A great example is when a cold Request for Proposal (RFP) comes in the mail. We've all gotten them, and many of us have responded to them – blindly."

"A cold RFP?" Frank wasn't sure what The Wizard meant by the term.

"Yes," explained The Wizard, "an RFP that lands on your desk with little or no warning from the potential customer. You immediately call the prospective customer and ask to meet with them, and they tell you they can't meet with you because if they meet with you they will have to meet with everyone. And they just don't have the time to invest in meeting with everyone."

"So, what they are saying is that they are not willing to invest in you," said Frank, tying in the learnings from earlier in the day.

"Given the fact they are not willing to invest in you, what do you think the odds are that you will win the contract?" asked The Wizard.

"How about ten to one against," offered Frank, building off The Wizard's earlier statistics. "I guess if you understand the Buying/Decision Process, if we didn't bring the prospective customer to *Identification of Needs*, then someone else did and they are sitting in the catbird seat."

"Exactly," agreed The Wizard. "Your only hope is if the customer is willing to meet with you, and through *SIGN* questions you are able to help them understand their needs in a new or different way."

"In the *Resolve Concerns* stage the customer has typically already made the decision to purchase and has some remaining issues that need to be resolved." The Wizard continued.

"The consultative salesperson acting as a Trusted Advisor can create value in this stage by helping the customer resolve concerns in a way that makes him feel comfortable with his decision."

The Wizard continued to explain the rest of the Buying/ Decision Process. "The next stage is the *Purchase* stage. In this stage, you must make the purchase as easy as possible. It is critical for the customer to know that you have the necessary influence within your own company to make things happen. Now is not the time for credit applications – all of that should have been done earlier."

"The final stage is the *Implement/Use* stage," said The Wizard. "In this stage, the consultative salesperson can share issues, problems and pitfalls based on experience with previous implementations and experiences that can benefit the customer."

"So that's it?" asked Frank. "That's the entire customer Buying/Decision Process? It seems simple enough."

"Oh, it's simple enough, all right. But now we need to overlay sales activities so that the entire process comes to life," explained The Wizard. "Bringing a customer to *Identification of Needs* is not a one-time event. It is an ongoing process of continually creating value by helping customers understand their needs in a new or different way."

The Wizard drew a line on the whiteboard, from the Implement/Use stage of the Buying/Decision Process back to the *Identification of Needs* stage, illustrating a continuous loop in creating value for customers.

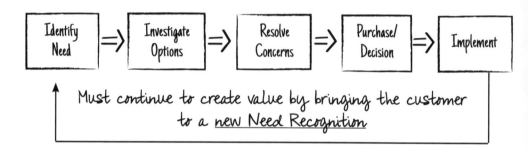

"At the end of the day, the customer pays you for the services and/or products," explained The Wizard. "Once the sale is complete, I say you're even. You have to earn your keep all over again, every single day, by bringing the customer to *Identification of Needs* stage before your competitors have an opportunity to do so."

"That makes perfect sense," agreed Frank. "Too many of us become complacent just because we solved a customer problem and closed a sale six months or a year ago and we think the customer owes us his undying loyalty. If I understand this process correctly, we need to constantly help our customers solve their problems, helping them to understand their needs in a new or different way."

"Exactly! Over time, things can – and do – change. You can have new key decision makers, new key decision influencers, changing priorities, changing technology or a specific compelling event driving change," expounded The Wizard. "If you go in with the idea that you have to continue to create value for your customers and work constantly to bring them to *Identification of Needs*, you should never lose a customer."

"Is that what you did, Jack?" asked Frank.

"I would like to think so. I wouldn't be teaching this process if I didn't believe in it," answered The Wizard.

"Now we need to move on to combining the Sales Process with the Buying/Decision Process to tie the two processes together."

Chapter 6: Merging the Sales Process With the Buying/Decision Process

Now it was up to The Wizard to tie it all together from a Sales/Buying/Decision Process standpoint.

He and Frank had earlier discussed the typical sales process used by most companies. They reviewed why it was often unsuccessful, primarily due to their internal focus on generating leads and "closing" for business. The Wizard had a very methodical and consistent approach for building a portfolio of prospective customers and trying to stay top of mind with those customers to enable him to bring them to *Identification of Needs*.

"Okay, Frank, let's start to tie the sales process to the Buying/Decision Process to get this whole thing to make sense," said The Wizard. "Earlier, we talked in terms of the steps of the sales cycle: Prospecting, Qualifying, Customer Meetings, etc. I would like to propose to you that you segment your customer/prospect database by how you can create value for them. Once that is complete, you need to target a specific set of prospects that you will contact on a regular basis. I would suggest reaching out to them a minimum of once per month. This can be done via voicemail, e-mail, phone, or face-to-face. Your objective is to stay 'top of mind' with your prospects. By contacting them on a regular basis, you are accomplishing two things. First, you are familiarizing them with your name as well as your company's brand.

...if they are 100% satisfied with their current suppliers, you are building brand with your potential customers as one who is committed to doing business with them."

"How many times should you contact the prospect before moving on?" asked Frank. "I don't want to waste my time if the customer won't see me."

"Good question, Frank. 100% of sales people call once, 80% call twice and 25% call three times. In other words, there is a huge drop-off after two contacts. I would suggest that you make a commitment of eighteen touches - that is, one and a half years of trying to stay top of mind before removing a qualified prospect from your database."

"What do you mean by a qualified prospect?" asked Frank.

"I mean a regular user and/or decision maker of the products and services you sell. By staying with the prospect for eighteen months, you will be able to see any seasonality associated with the business, and there is a better than 40% chance there will be a change in prospect personnel during the eighteen-month period, which can work to your advantage."

The Wizard continued, "As you can see by the illustration on the board, all of your activities are designed to keep you top of mind with your customer or prospect.

Creating Value for the Customer

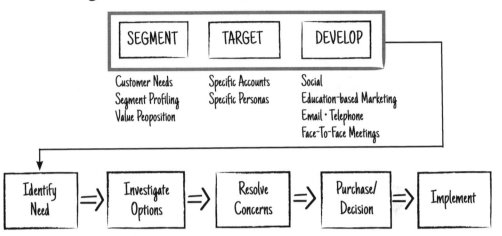

You funnel all your activities for one reason, and one reason only…"

Frank interrupted, "So what you are saying is that all the activities and everything I do is designed to bring a customer to an *Identification of Needs*, correct?"

Frank felt good about his progress in understanding the process. The Wizard had spent the full the day with him. Frank felt that the relationship side of the business was a big factor in how he did business with his customers, and yet The Wizard had spent little time talking about relationships. Frank was curious how The Wizard was going to portray the relationship side of the business in the ensuing discussion.

Frank decided to bring up the relationship discussion, but before he could get the word out of his mouth The Wizard said, "Now, we move on to the relationship side of consultative selling."

Understanding Customer Relationships

The Wizard walked over to the whiteboard and picked up a marker. "Customer relationships, like most relationships, can be likened to a pyramid broken into three distinct sections: the top, the middle and the bottom," said The Wizard as he drew on the whiteboard.

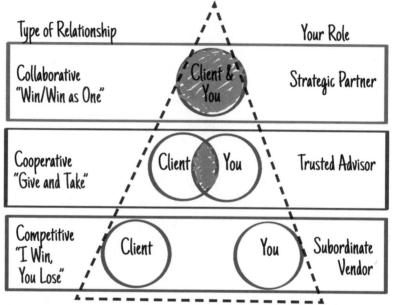

"The bottom third of the pyramid is what I call the competitive relationship. Here the customer and the supplier are most polarized. The role the supplier plays is one of a subordinate vendor to the customer. In this scenario, the customer typically wins and the supplier typically loses. These are the type of relationships where the supplier gives, gives, gives, gives, gives and the customer takes, takes, takes. The customer usually sees the supplier as readily replaceable and changes suppliers on a regular basis."

"I know the type of relationship you are talking about," interjected Frank. "I have a couple of customers that get a real thrill out of pulling me through the wringer. I just never thought of it in terms you are describing."

"What would you propose to do with customer relationships that are classified as competitive?" asked The Wizard.

"Obviously, I would like to move them up the pyramid to at least a cooperative level, where the customer would see me as a person who can create value for them as a Trusted Advisor," replied Frank as he began to more fully understand the relationship pyramid.

"And if you could not move them to the cooperative level in a set period of time?" asked The Wizard.

"Then I guess I would have to exit the relationship," Frank said thoughtfully. He had in mind at least two customers he could fire, but he thought they might benefit from seeing the relationship pyramid and ask where they saw their relationship before he terminated that relationship. "Did you ever think of sharing the relationship pyramid with one of your competitive customers?"

"Absolutely!" replied The Wizard, without batting an eye. "Anytime I made a customer presentation, one of the first slides I would show was the relationship pyramid. You would be amazed how many times the customers I viewed as competitive viewed the relationship as cooperative!"

"Really! What usually happened when they saw the difference of opinion?"

"In most cases, the customer – understanding my perception of the relationship – either shared more information with me about why he behaved the way he did or simply changed behaviors. I don't believe there are all that many customers that truly want to be bucketed in a competitive relationship. Some are trained that way. Others are just not aware of how they treat suppliers."

"It probably makes sense to use the relationship pyramid early in the process so that you can level-set expectations with the customers, don't you think?" suggested Frank.

"That's good thinking, Frank. As I said earlier today, you only have 525,600 minutes in a year, and every minute you invest in a competitive relationship that is not moving up the pyramid is a minute you don't have to invest in a cooperative or collaborative one."

"That's so true, Jack," acknowledged Frank. He was thinking about his cooperative and collaborative customer relationships and realizing that he had to prioritize the time he was able to spend with them. "I assume you are going to share with me the characteristics of the cooperative and collaborative relationships."

"Yes, I am. Let's move on to the cooperative relationship, which is categorized by give and take. Sometimes you give, sometimes for the greater good the customer gives. You both understand each other's importance. There is mutual respect. Customers look to you for subject matter expertise and trust you will act in their best interests. They look to you as a 'go-to' person to help solve their problems. The relationship is win-win. Your role is one of a Trusted Advisor. The top sales people typically have about 80% of their customer relationships in this category."

"I believe I have several customers that would fall into this area." Frank felt good that he was able to say that with confidence. "Have you ever lost a customer that you considered you had a good, cooperative relationship with?"

"Yes, Frank, I have. Before I truly understood the Buying/Decision Process and my impact on it, I lost a very good cooperative customer because I was asleep at the switch!"

"Another supplier brought them to *Identification of Needs*?" asked Frank innocently.

"Exactly!" recalled The Wizard. "The customer was one I had been doing business with for three years. One day, my sponsor came to me and asked me if my company had an electronic requisitioning system via the Internet. He said they were tired of pushing paper-based requisitions. Of course, we did not have an electronic requisitioning system at the time. I told the customer I would look into it and get back to him. Just like an ostrich that sticks his head in the sand, I waited for this request to blow over. Three months later, I was called into the office of the customer's new VP of Operations. My day-to-day sponsor was there with a gloomy look on his face, and the VP proceeded to tell me they were moving their business to a competitor based on their electronic requisitioning system and overall distribution capability."

"Ouch!" sympathized Frank. "That must have hurt."

"It was a crushing blow," confessed The Wizard. "Yes, losing the business sure hurt. But I think the biggest loss was seeing the look on my sponsor's face, knowing he had given me every opportunity to provide the solution, and yet, I just plain let him down. I vowed that would never happen again…and it never did!"

"I had heard that you never lost a customer. At least that's what the legend of The Wizard says."

"Well, I am telling you firsthand. I don't know of any salesperson who has not lost a customer at one time or another – including me. You see, Frank, I learned that when customers ask you questions about features or functionality, or just shares problems with you, the behavior is typically driven by a need. Either something has changed internally, or another supplier has created an *Identification of Needs* with your customer. When your customer asks you a question like my former customer asked me, don't stick your head in the sand and hope it will go away. Start asking questions to see what is driving the need, explore alternatives, and use it as an opportunity to create your own *Identification of Needs* with the customer. Keep in mind, there are different levels of cooperative relationships and the level of cooperation by the customer is directly proportional to the value you can create for them."

"I see," said Frank. "Again, your teachings are amazingly consistent and tie together unbelievably well. I am really anxious to understand the collaborative relationship and why there are such a small number of those types of relationships with customers."

The Wizard then began to address the third component of the pyramid, which was the top third. "Collaborative relationships are where you are so aligned that you almost can't tell the buyer from the seller. You are viewed as a strategic thought partner, one with access to knowledge and resources designed to help your customer improve business performance."

"Strategic Thought Partner? Improved business performance? I must say I am a little bit lost," confessed Frank.

The Wizard paused to collect his thoughts and began to speak again. "In a collaborative relationship, your goals are so aligned that one does not distinguish the buyer from the seller. One only sees a problem as an opportunity and marshals the necessary resources to create maximum value for both. Your goal is improved business performance on behalf of your customer. The customer wants to leverage all the resources you and your company can bring to bear in order to achieve his goals. The relationship is categorized by respect, trust, and subject matter expertise."

"That sounds like the perfect relationship," declared

Frank. "Why wouldn't you want 80% of your customers in the collaborative relationship?"

"Because the customer expects such extraordinary value creation from the supplier and utilizes all the resources the supplier has available. This can be very time-consuming, and you can only manage a couple of these types of relationships at a time. They are extremely profitable, long-term, resource-depleting and time-consuming," explained The Wizard. "Most companies do not have the maturity to maintain these types of relationships with suppliers, and quite frankly, most suppliers lack the integrity and commitment to manage these types of relationships as well."

"That makes sense," agreed Frank. "If you don't mind me asking, at the peak of your career, how many of these types of relationships did you have going on at any given time?"

"At the peak of my career," shared The Wizard, "I had three collaborative relationships and seven cooperative relationships going on at once."

"Ten accounts? That's it?" That didn't sound like much to Frank. "I manage over thirty accounts today."

"Yes, Frank, ten accounts," conceded The Wizard. "But those ten accounts comprised over $50 million in annual sales, and the three accounts I would consider to be 'collaborative' made up close to $30 million of that."

Frank's jaw dropped. He was speechless. He was floored by the number The Wizard had just shared with him.

He had no idea. He knew The Wizard was the most successful salesperson in the history of Standard, but he had no idea that his personal sales topped $50 million annually. Frank knew that even today, the top salesperson at Standard came in slightly less than $15 million, and that Al had a legitimate shot at being the #1 person at Standard this year at that revenue level."

"Fifty million," gasped Frank. He was not quite sure how to respond. "I had no idea you did that kind of business."

"Most people have no idea," shared The Wizard. "People forgot about the number over the years and gave me The Wizard nickname instead. As you can see, it kind of stuck."

"And today, everything you shared with me is what you used to become the legend you are today?" Frank now had a true appreciation of this man, who had invested the entire day sharing his approach to selling in today's marketplace.

"Yes, Frank. What I shared with you today is how I went to market and how I teach people to sell consultatively today."

"I don't know how to thank you for your investment in me," said a very humbled Frank.

"Be the successful salesperson you are capable of being, Frank," said The Wizard. "Develop successful habits. Create value for your customers. And I will be watching for you on the President's Roundtable."

"Yes…the President's Roundtable." Frank allowed himself to daydream a bit until The Wizard interrupted.

"Frank, it's time for us to wrap-up our Lessons Learned."

The Wizard's Lessons Learned

At the whiteboard again, The Wizard said to Frank, "Starting with the four cornerstones that Al shared with you, please write down your key learnings in your own words."

Frank walked over to the whiteboard, took the dry erase marker and summarized his key learnings.

Frank's Key Learnings

1. Attitude is the start of everything — find the ice skates in life

2. Personal Accountability — buy a mirror

3. Perseverance — I must strive for progressive improvement, faster than my competition

4. I must develop good habits and eliminate bad habits

5. Listen — I must seek to understand before asking to be understood

6. Prescription before diagnosis equals malpractice

7. I must be in the customer's operating reality in order to truly find the pain

8. I must use the Call Planning Worksheet to effectively plan my sales calls

9. I must understand the Buying/Decision Process and create an Identification of Needs

10. I must use effective SIGN questioning to create GAP

11. Objections are merely a request for more information – LAER

12. I must understand that all sales activities are designed to keep me top of mind with the customer in an effort to create an ongoing Identification of Needs

13. I must work to move up the relationship pyramid: Competitive, Cooperative, Collaborative

The Wizard was pleased with what Frank had put on the board, demonstrating that he had acquired a clear understanding of the material they had covered. His only hope was that Frank would be able to effectively execute his key learnings by making them a part of his regular routine.

As the time approached 5:00 PM, Frank was amazed at how much ground he and The Wizard had covered in one day. He felt energized by the teachings The Wizard had shared with him. He knew this day would be a defining moment in his life and his career. He knew he had just received priceless training from one of the greatest sales people he had ever met. He thought about his friend Al and how nice it was of him to share his mentor. But most of all, he asked himself how could he possible repay Jack Anderson, the man simply known to most as The Wizard?

Frank turned away from the board and turned towards

The Wizard, extending his right hand, "Thank you so much for today, Jack Anderson. I now know why you are called The Wizard. I will never forget the investment you made in me today."

"The pleasure was all mine," replied The Wizard. "I enjoyed getting to know you better and sharing my experiences with you. I am certain that if you apply what you have learned here today, you will undoubtedly do great things! And I will be watching."

"I am shooting for the President's Roundtable!" declared Frank, knowing he had nine full months to qualify. The day had given him newfound optimism that he could get himself there.

I will look forward to seeing you there," said The Wizard, who was an honorary member of the President's Roundtable. "In fact, I'll be counting on it."

The Wizard walked him to the door and bid his new friend farewell. There, the old bull and the young bull stood, each knowing that today they had actually helped each other. Frank received a priceless education on consultative selling, and Jack Anderson got to do what he did best – share his life experiences with an up-and-coming young bull. The two men shook hands and bid each other farewell.

As he walked down the steps of The Wizard's building and onto the sidewalk, Frank decided to take the subway back downtown to Battery Park. "Subways are 98% on time," he thought to himself. "I should only be so good."

Chapter 7: Putting It All Together

The next morning, Frank woke up with renewed energy and purpose. He wanted to do a million things at once. He decided the first thing he needed to do was to call his good friend, Al, and thank him for arranging the meeting with The Wizard. Next, he would pick up a thank you card and some sort of gift for The Wizard to show at least a small token of his appreciation.

Frank was still marveling at what an unbelievable experience he had shared with The Wizard the day before. The man's clarity of purpose, ability to break down complex issues as part of a process, and his consistency in approach was unmatched by any other sales training Frank had ever been through. The Wizard's relentless commitment to staying in the customer's operating reality was clearly a new and improved way of doing business that Frank could implement to his – and his customer's benefit. Frank made a commitment to himself that very moment, he would change. He began by making copies of the list he had formulated for The Wizard on the whiteboard. One copy was for his desk, one for his portfolio, and one for his home office. He now understood that his future in sales would start today and that he was going to make the most of it.

The smell of fresh coffee finished brewing and the clock struck seven, as Frank began his new career by reviewing his customer/prospect database to make sure there was alignment. As he went through the list of contacts, he made notes designating each relationship as competitive, cooperative or collaborative. He then began planning his calls for the day and for the week. "Things are going to be different from now on," he said, making a commitment to himself.

Frank arrived at the office just before 8:30 AM. Pam had already been there for an hour and was anxious to learn how Frank's day with the Wizard had gone.

"Good morning Frank," Pam said clearly excited to see him. "How did the day with The Wizard go yesterday? It was yesterday, wasn't it?"

"Yes, it was yesterday," acknowledged Frank. "It was awesome. I learned so much about process and customer relationships. I just wish I hadn't had to wait nearly three years to see him. I mean, I basically wasted three years when I could have had all this great knowledge from the beginning."

"No, you didn't," argued Pam.

"Yes, I did," replied Frank. He wondered why Pam would make such a statement.

"You don't understand, Frank. He would never have seen you prior to this."

"What? What do you mean he wouldn't have seen me? Al arranged this meeting, and if Al had asked for the meeting earlier, I am sure he would have seen me," countered Frank. He firmly believed Al could have gotten him in to see The Wizard anytime he wanted to.

"Wrong," said Pam, in a confident and experienced tone. There are a number of things that have to happen before The Wizard will see you."

"Oh, yeah, like what?" asked Frank. He was sure that Pam did not know the answer to his question.

"First, you have to have a minimum of three years' sales experience. The Wizard wants people to have been around the block a few times before he commits to spending a day with them."

"Well, I don't have three full years of experience," responded Frank.

"You have 33 months, close enough," Pam pointed out. "Secondly, you have to be a high potential person as defined by the person sponsoring you. And the sponsor has to be a President's Roundtable member. In your case, Al is your sponsor, and it is critical he provides you with a thorough understanding of the four cornerstones before you can see The Wizard. And finally, you must be coming off of a huge loss or be at a coachable moment – meaning you are ready to make the necessary adjustments to your approach."

"Wow." Frank was impressed with her grasp of the requirements. "Well, I certainly qualified by that last criterion – in spades!"

"So, you learned a lot?" asked Pam.

"Yes, I did. The best thing is, I learned it in such a logical sequence that I don't think that I will ever forget it."

"Have you spoken to Al yet?" asked Pam.

The first thing on Frank's *To Do* list was to call Al and thank him for arranging the meeting. "I need to call Al now. Thanks for reminding me," Frank said to Pam as he began to scurry toward his desk.

"Don't mention it." Pam smiled. She could already see the change in Frank.

Frank dialed Al's number and waited nervously for Al to answer. He was very appreciative of what Al had done for him and wanted to make sure he thanked him properly.

"Good morning, Al Marion speaking," said the familiar voice that answered the phone.

"Al, good morning, it's Frank."

"Frank, my man, how you doin'? How did it go yesterday with The Wizard?"

"I am doing great," Frank responded. "I thought the meeting yesterday went very well. I think we really connected, and I learned a lot."

"He said the same thing. He thought you had a tremendous amount of potential and had no doubt that if you stuck with the plan, you would be a President's Roundtable member in no time at all," Al recounted, remembering the conversation he had the previous evening with The Wizard.

"Well, that's great to hear," sighed a relieved Frank. "I thought we hit it off well. But after the rough start we got off to, you never know."

Al responded quickly with, "You were late, weren't you?"

"How did you know?" Frank wondered if The Wizard told him.

"You said you had a rough start, and I assumed you were late – because you told me you are never late," reminded Al.

"Never say never – it's the kiss of death," they both said at the same time laughing.

"Al," Frank began, "I just wanted to say how much I appreciate what you did for me by arranging the day with The Wizard. I mean, I have never had such focused, one-on-one training in my life. It truly meant a lot to me."

"Don't mention it, Frank. I had selfish reasons for doing what I did," confessed Al. "I want my good friend and former teammate beside me on the President's Roundtable. I know you can get there, because if I can do it, you can do it!"

"I am sure with the Reliant deal, you will be the next Director of the President's Roundtable!" exclaimed Frank, so very proud of his mentor.

"One day at a time, my friend," cautioned Al. "There is still a lot of the year left and anything can happen."

"You will make it happen, Al," said a confident and proud Frank.

"I'll make a deal with you, Frank," offered Al. "I will win the Directorship if you make a commitment to me that you will make the Roundtable. Deal?"

"Well, Al, I don't know," said a cautiously optimistic Frank, knowing he had a long way to go if he was ever going to make something like that happen.

"Is it a deal or isn't it?" Asked Al in a forceful tone.

"It's a deal," acquiesced Frank. "I will somehow figure out a way to make it happen."

"Great, I need to be at Reliant by nine for an Expectations Meeting. I'll give you a call later to discuss your experience with The Wizard in detail," offered Al.

"No problem, Al. I'll talk to you later."

The two men hung up the phone and went about their respective activities. Al was off to Reliant to make sure his new account was implemented correctly under his "start right, stay right" methodology. Frank set off to use his newfound skills exactly the way The Wizard had taught him.

Frank knew he still had nine months left in the year and that he could conceivably achieve the commitment he had made to Al. But he also knew it would take focus, rigor and discipline to make it happen. Only time would tell....

Chapter 8: Becoming the Only Choice

Three Months Later...

After taking on Al's challenge and working hard to develop all of the successful habits The Wizard had taught him, things began to change for Frank. He was more confident in his abilities, and his customers could see it. He was more diagnostically oriented, and his customers clearly understood that Frank was truly trying to help them improve their business performance rather than just going for a quick sale.

About a month after Frank left The Wizard, he scheduled a follow-up meeting with his contact at The Wheeler Company. He thought to himself, "This time, things are going to be different!" And of course, they WERE!

Frank did a thorough job of researching The Wheeler Company before he returned for second visit, gaining a basic understanding of the company and its products. He clearly understood which products were growing and which ones were declining. He planned his sales call using the Call Planning Worksheet and developed his *SIGN* questions. He listed possible customer questions and objections, all the while keeping himself in the customer's *operating reality*.

He had a great meeting and was able to arrange a *Discovery* to assess and go even deeper into the issues that existed in Wheeler's operation. Frank was also able to – using his new planning, preparation and relationship building skills – arrange a final presentation proposing a three-year agreement worth just shy of $2.5 million annually. And today was the big day.

Frank's big meeting at Wheeler got started right on time, at 9:00 AM. In the weeks leading up to the presentation, Frank had done all the things The Wizard had trained him to do. In his early meetings with Wheeler and through a series of prepared *SIGN* questions, he was able to uncover needs the customer had that were not being met in its current environment and by its current suppliers. He had a clear understanding of the customer's operation, objectives and how his proposed program would align with the company's objectives.

As for the presentation itself, he was able to get in the room the day before the meeting to make sure everything was set up perfectly. He even did a practice demonstration of his company's technology using Wheeler's intranet, making sure everything worked.

As the meeting began, Frank took the time to introduce himself, and to be sure he knew all the players in the room. He started the presentation by thanking all of them for taking time out of their busy schedules to invest time in him and the Standard Company.

Next, he provided a chronological overview of his research efforts. Frank then listed critical concerns and objectives of the group that he had been able to uncover making sure the list included a representation of each of their concerns. To test for understanding and agreement, he used his patented response checking methodology, saying, "Is this list of critical concerns and objectives consistent with what you gave me during the Discovery process?"

After the Wheeler associates acknowledged that Frank had the correct issues on the board, he clearly demonstrated to the group that there was *GAP* between their desired program and the actual state of their program. By looking at the gap through the customer's eyes, meaning that he was in the customer's *operating reality*, Frank clearly demonstrated empathy for their concerns. Next, Frank helped them explore and evaluate their options and – acting as a 'trusted advisor' – helped to resolve their concerns.

Several of the Wheeler people began to ask questions about what the next steps would be and how to go forward with Frank and the Standard Company. Frank could tell that the team of people at Wheeler were feeling confident that Frank and the solution he and the Standard Company provided could meet their needs. Frank's hard work had positioned Standard as the only choice.

Frank asked for a letter of intent, to be delivered as soon as possible, and told the assembled team that he would like to arrange an Expectations Meeting and an Implementation meeting during the next 30 days.

"If we are all in agreement, I'll email Frank the letter of intent this afternoon," said Steve Livingston, the Vice President of Operations for Wheeler, as all the members of his team nodded in agreement. "Would that be enough to get you started as we work out the details of the contract?"

"That would be perfect," replied Frank. "How about next Tuesday for the Expectations Meeting?" The Wheeler team agreed to meet with Frank again the following Tuesday.

Frank made his rounds, shook each person's hand from Wheeler and thanked them for their commitment and their faith in Standard. As the clients left the room, he turned his attention to his team: Mike from Marketing, Tony from Finance, Gail from Human Resources, Larry from Information Technology, and Fred, his District Manager.

Frank began by saying, "I want to thank each and every one of you for your help and support during the Discovery process, and for helping me make sure this presentation was flawless. And I want to thank you in advance for a similar outcome at the Expectations and Implementation meetings. Business is a team sport and no one can do it alone. You all need to know that we could not have achieved this huge customer win without the efforts and insights of each and every one of you! Please accept my sincere appreciation for a job well done."

His teammates all shook hands, high-fived and hugged each other. It was a huge win, and one the whole team could be proud of. As he started to shut things down and put the projector back in its case, Frank thought to himself, "Thank you, Mr. Wizard, for investing in me and showing me how it's done. I could never have done this without you."

Just then, Frank remembered that he needed to call The Wizard right away to arrange a time to drop off the gift he had ordered for him. He was excited about the opportunity to talk with The Wizard again and to share with him the news about the Wheeler deal. *"The Wizard will be proud,"* thought Frank.

One Year Later: Paradise Island, The Bahamas

On a beautiful sunny day in the Bahamas, a big, blue, chartered bus pulled up to the prestigious Atlantis Hotel and Casino. In line with company custom, a line of Standard Company's executive leaders and company officers awaited the arrival of their top sales people.

As the bus door swung open and the sales people stepped off, the tropical music that had accompanied the sales team from the airport wafted through the door. As they came off the bus, each team member was greeted by a company officer, and handed a tropical drink as a lei was put around their neck, welcoming them to the 100 Plus Club. An honor reserved for sales people who had achieved 100% of their quota with a minimum of 15% sales and profit growth over the prior year.

It was a *Who's Who* of talented sales people. As the bus emptied, people greeted each other with hugs and handshakes, and the energy and optimism reached a fevered pitch.

Just then, a long, black stretch limousine began to slowly part the crowd. Everyone turned to look – they knew that the stretch limo held the elite of the elite sales force –The President's Roundtable members, who are notified of their status at the airport, just before they board their flight to the 100 Plus Club. Not until they have all arrived and are tucked in the limo do they find out who their Director is.

In accordance with custom, the newest member of the Roundtable exited the limousine first. This year's newest member and first-time President's Roundtable member goes by the name of Frank Kelly. Yes, it is true! Frank lived up to his commitment to Al and to the expectations of The Wizard, finding his way to the President's Roundtable. After a performance of 83% of quota in the first half of the year, Frank ended the second half of the year by signing three new customer contracts and finishing the year at 145% of quota, his efforts earning him his first 100 Plus Club Award. Frank was beaming as he exited the limo.

As he worked his way through the crowd, there was one person that Frank was anxious to see – the honorary Chairman of the President's Roundtable, a man named Jack Anderson – or, as his friends called him, The Wizard. Frank caught a glimpse of Jack as he was congratulating Mary Ann Panlin on her 15th straight 100 Plus Club. Frank and The Wizard made eye contact just as the trumpets began to sound, the signal that the identity of the Director was about to be announced.

Finally, the last person in the limo was about to step out and be welcomed to the 100 Plus Club. Everyone turned to see who this year's top salesperson was – the Director of the President's Roundtable. Frank made his way over to The Wizard as he watched the Director step out of the limousine. The crowd of happy sales people all stood and applauded as Al Marion stepped onto the pavement while toasting the crowd with margarita in hand. Frank and The Wizard smiled as Al stepped out of the limo and waved to his fellow sales people.

"This must be a real thrill for you," Frank said to The Wizard. "None of this could have happened without you! Even though I've said thank you at least ten times already, I would like to thank you again."

"Frank, the pleasure has truly been all mine. Honestly, you have no idea how rewarding it is for me to see what you and Al have accomplished."

Standard's Vice President of Sales chose that moment to come over to shake hands with Jack and Frank, congratulating Frank on a great year and almost genuflecting to The Wizard, respectful of and grateful for the service he had provided to the company over the years.

"I have my eyes on you, Frank Kelly," said the Vice President of Sales. "People tell me you will make a great sales manager one day. They say you have a real talent for coaching people on how to elicit customer needs and wants. I hear you do a great job framing the Standard offerings to meet those customer needs. We can use people like you in sales management at Standard."

"Thank you, sir; I appreciate the vote of confidence." Frank was both surprised and flattered by the recognition he had just received.

"Let's get together sometime over the next three or four days and explore some of the possibilities that might exist," said the Vice President of Sales.

"I would like that very much, sir," replied Frank.

As the Vice President of Sales turned his attention toward Al Marion and the larger crowd, Frank turned to The Wizard and asked, "What do you know about sales management?"

The Wizard looked at Frank and smiled. "I might know a thing or two," he said. The two men burst into laughter as they made their way through the crowd toward Al Marion, the newly crowned Director of the President's Roundtable.

To Be Continued.

Glossary

Active Listening - Listening to understand rather than merely listening to hear.

Call Planning Worksheet - A document used to pre-plan a sales call. The document contains basic account information and sales strategy planning including account name and contact, primary and secondary objectives, SIGN questions, anticipated objections, etc. A Call Planning Worksheet should be completed in preparation for any face-to-face customer interaction.

Discovery - An in depth set of diagnostics on a customer's current situation, including process mapping in an effort to gain a greater understanding of opportunities for improvement. Sometimes referred to as an Assessment.

LAER - An acronym for Listen, Acknowledge, Explore, and Respond, which is a process used for effectively handling customer objections.

Muscle Memory - A term used primarily in sports for reacting without thinking. In business, it refers to developing outstanding habits in an effort to do the right thing automatically without having to give a great deal of thought.

Operating Reality - The ability to see problems and opportunities as they appear through the customer's eyes.

Identify Needs - Also referred to Identification of Needs. The first stage of a customer's Buying/Decision Process. It is the first time a customer understands there is a GAP between desired state and actual state and looks for a product, program or service to meet those needs.

SIGN Questions - Situation, Insight, GAP and Needs/Solution questions.

Strategic Thought Partner - A perception by the customer, usually in collaborative relationships, whereby the customer believes the salesperson bring subject matter expertise, strong problem-solving skills and vision to the relationship and can bring the necessary resources to the customer to help improve business performance.

Trusted Advisor - A perception the customer has of the value the salesperson brings to the relationship. It is typically based on the salesperson's ability to demonstrate empathy, subject matter expertise and to see problems and opportunities in the customer's operating reality.